W9-CCI-714

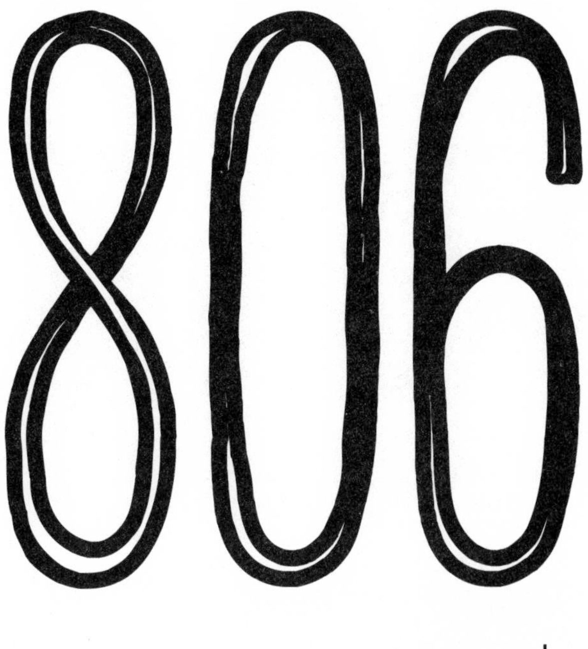

a novel

BY CYNTHIA WEIL

Tanglewood • Indianapolis

Published by Tanglewood Publishing, Inc.

Cover Design by Karina Granda
Interior Design by Amy Alick Perich

Tanglewood Publishing, Inc.
1060 N. Capitol Ave., Ste. E-395
Indianapolis, IN 46204
www.tanglewoodbooks.com

Printed in U.S.A.
10 9 8 7 6 5 4 3 2 1

ISBN 978-1-939100-14-6

Library of Congress Cataloging-in-Publication Data

Names: Weil, Cynthia, author.
Title: 806 : a novel / Cynthia Weil.
Other titles: Eight oh six
Description: Indianapolis, IN : Tanglewood, [2018] | Summary: KT, sixteen, learns that her father was Donor 806, discovers two half-brothers, and travels with them from Missouri to California to meet their biological father, redefining their notions of "family" along the way.
Identifiers: LCCN 2017031596 <tel:2017031596> | ISBN 9781939100146 (hardcover)
Subjects: | CYAC: Identity--Fiction. | Sperm donors--Fiction. | Mothers and daughters--Fiction. | Brothers and sisters--Fiction. | Automobile travel--Fiction. | Single-parent families--Fiction.
Classification: LCC PZ7.1.W43 Aah 2018 | DDC [Fic]--dc23
LC record available at https://lccn.loc.gov/2017031596

To my family, for being
everything I need and love.

prologue

To: DSC.org
From: NonameBand@aol.com
Subject: Successes and Failures
Date: July 17, 2008

Your website says that you want to know about successes and failures that have come about from using the website, so I'm writing to tell you about me.

Contacting DSC.org was the scariest thing I've ever done, but it changed my life, so I'm sending you my story. Even though it's probably way too long to post, and you actually may know a little bit of it, (you'll see what I mean when you get near the end), I wanted to write to you because I realize how much I owe you. Without your help, I never would have found out who I am. So, along with my story, I am sending you a big, fat thank you.

Yours sincerely,
Katherine Lambert

chapter one

My mom, Kim, looks a lot like Reese Witherspoon, if Reese wore a Burger Boy manager's uniform. But in spite of that, she's lost every man she's ever loved or thought she loved, beginning with my father, who dumped her when I was just a baby bump. The day she lost Bruce, her latest boyfriend, kind of pushed me over the edge, but it turned out to be the beginning of everything.

On the day the Bruce thing happened—June 13, 2008, to be exact—I was actually feeling sort of happy because it was the last day of school. My school, Central High in St. Louis, had the garden variety mix of cheerleaders, popular kids, jocks, freaks, nerds, goths, and druggies sprinkled with some G wannabees and a few genuine OGs who had never been able to pass something or other and would no doubt advance to be AGs (ancient gangsters) before they managed to graduate.

Then, in a category all our own, there was yours truly and Sasha Greene. She was my best (and actually, my only) friend and the drummer in our band, Noname. Sasha and I kind of looked alike. We both had black hair with blue streaks, and we both got the blue dye at CrazyHair.com. The only difference was that her hair was dark, so she had to bleach some of it for the blue dye to take. My hair is actually blond, so I had to dye and tone.

But back to my story. When I got home from school that day, I was a little freaked out to see Mom's car parked outside our garden apartment because she usually does payroll on Friday and rolls in around 7:00 p.m.

I walked in the kitchen door and knew right away what was going down when I heard my mom and Bruce arguing in the living room. In times like these, and there have been more of them than I can count, I began to think of my mom as "Kim" instead of "Mom" because she would act like such a kid. I even called her Kim sometimes, which she pretended not to notice. Whoever said "history repeats itself" must have known my mother intimately. I knew this discussion by heart, only the names of the men involved changed.

I would have bet my last guitar pick that Bruce had texted her at work, saying they had to talk, and she had insisted that they see each other, like immediately.

When someone says "we have to talk," even though you know they're not going to talk about anything good, for some strange reason, you absolutely have to hear what they have to say ASAP.

I used to fantasize about making Mom sit down and write "nobody likes needy" a thousand times and paste the paper on her bathroom mirror. Then she would see it every day and possibly remember it when the next "one" came along.

I could hear their voices clearly through the wall, even though I didn't want to. I figured if I made a smoothie, the sound of the blender would drown them out. So I opened the fridge, which was filled with Burger Boy food (I find that stuff seriously disgusting), and pulled out yogurt, orange juice, and strawberries for a healthy, soothing, (and I hoped) calming beverage.

The dialogue coming through was so loud and so clear that the noisy blender didn't stand a chance.

"Kim, it's not you, it's me," Bruce insisted. "I'm not good enough for you."

"That line was a whole episode of that sitcom 'about nothing.' It didn't work there, and it doesn't work here."

"But it's true, Kimmy. I swear."

"You know 'good' makes me feel bad about myself. I don't want 'good.' I want you," she said in her little girl voice, which I found embarrassing and sad.

That last statement shook me up on so many levels, I had to roll my eyes even though there was no one there to see it. I was so bummed that I almost forgot to put ice cubes in the blender. This could have led to a warm smoothie crisis, but it was easily fixable. I took a few out of the freezer with a flourish and popped them in. That's when I heard Bruce, his voice half annoyed and half guilty, saying, "I'm not as mature as you, Kimmy. I'm just not really ready for marriage."

"It was a suggestion, not an ultimatum," my mom explained. "I mean, I was actually trying to find out the level of your commitment."

That in itself was so was so lame I almost cried.

Bruce just got more annoyed. "I'm not ready to settle down. The truth is, I need to find myself."

Then I heard my mom clear her throat, which she always did before putting on her make-believe "tough" voice. I don't know how she came up with it, but it sounded like a combination of an angry Cher and an indignant Miley Cyrus. She thought it was venomous, but truth be told, it wasn't very scary, just very weird.

"I think somebody saw you in Pittsburgh. Why don't you start looking there? Now!" she spat in that strange voice.

After the longest, quietest ten seconds ever, Bruce mumbled, "I better go."

I punched "blend" again and didn't even look up as he walked past me, headed for the back door. Then I hit the "off" button and poured some of the smoothie into my glass. He stopped and turned to me with a funny look on his face.

"Bye, Bruce," I said.

"It's Bob," he answered. "Uh, can I have my blender?"

I unplugged it, walked over to him, dumped the rest of the smoothie into his jacket pocket, and handed him the blender. He took it with a sheepish look that told me he knew he deserved the gift.

"Have a nice life," he said, almost like he meant it. Leaving a trail of smoothie drops, he slunk out the back door.

There were no sobs coming from the living room, but I knew my mom was holding them in. Part of me wanted to make her cry hard for screwing up again, part of me wanted to find a way to make her feel better, and another part of me just wanted to get into my room so I could pick up my guitar, write a song, and forget what a dumb life I had in the family department.

The minute I tiptoed into the living room, Kim looked up at me like a pooch who had just been left at the shelter.

"Bob's gone," she said.

"Surprise, surprise." I took a few steps toward my room.

She bit her lip, swung her chair around, and began clicking the keys on the computer. "What do you think about my changing to JDate?" she asked. "My mother always told me that Jewish men don't leave."

"Grandma was divorced three times."

"But none of them were Jewish."

"If she didn't take her own advice, why should you?"

She stopped typing. I should have just walked into my room right then, but, no, I had to twist the knife. I was sixteen, after all. So when she started with, "Do you know what he said?" I cut her right off.

"'It's not you, it's me,' a popular phrase around here favored by Kevin, Chris, Walter, and Tim," I announced. "I personally preferred Jerry's 'I love you more than life, but I feel suicidal,' and Gary's 'This isn't easy, but neither are you' was a close second."

She winced. "Thanks for running down my lousy romantic track record, Katie. I guess I don't feel bad enough for you."

"It's KT, Mom. I told you."

My mom sighed. "I thought KT was just for the band."

"No, Kim, it's not just for the band," I snapped. "It's my new name."

"That's a really mean tone, whatever your name is," she said in a shaky voice. "And this is not the time to use it." She was trying to say what she thought was "mom" stuff and failing miserably.

Then she just gave up, leaned forward with her elbows on her knees, and covered her face with her hands. Her blond hair fell around her face like a curtain. Something in me wanted to throw my arms around her and kiss the top of her head the way I did when I was ten, but I knew where that would take us, so I put down my smoothie and pulled up a chair close to her.

"Mom, I'm sorry I sounded mean. I don't understand why you think you have to be with someone to be complete. I didn't want to sound obnoxious, I just get so frustrated when I see you getting hurt over and over again."

"I know," said her muffled voice. "Me too."

"Remember when I wrote that song for you after Gary? You promised to sing it to yourself whenever these things happened."

She nodded.

"Remember the words?"

She shook her head. I leaned in close and started to sing to her.

"When you headed out that door
Betch ya thought I'd fall apart,
But you didn't break me, babe,
You only broke my heart."

Then she pushed back her hair and joined in, kind of half-hearted and off-key.

"So if you think you did me in,
You better think again.
The truth is there's no way you could be wronger.
Baby, you just made me stronger,
You made me stronger."

She smiled a sad but hopeful smile and blew her nose. "I'm going to remember that, Katie. I really am. From now on."

"I hope so," I said, and then I noticed her eyes drifting toward the computer screen.

"Oooo, look, honey, here's something interesting: 'Banker, homebody, looking for shiksa soulmate who likes cozy nights in front of the fireplace, good wine, fine dining, and . . .'"

I couldn't believe her. I was scared that I was going to lose it because I knew deep down inside she was never going to change, no matter how many songs I wrote for her. I just headed for my room.

"Katie, KT, sweetie, listen," she called after me. "I

know you need a dad, and I'm going to find one for you if it kills me."

"And me, too," I mumbled.

She was so not getting it. There was something I had wanted to say for a long time, but I hadn't because I didn't want to hurt her feelings. I just wanted to get her off JDate and shake up her world and maybe get even with her, just a little, for screwing up again. So I spit it out: "I am so done with listening to stuff like this. I don't want you to find a new father for me. I have a father, and I want to see him. I want to talk to Max."

Mom turned to look straight at me with her "remember I'm the mother" face.

"Listen to me, Katie," she said. "You know as well as I do that he never tried to make any contact with us after he left. He moved away for years. He never called or wrote or tried to—"

"Do you know where he is?"

She swallowed, coughed, and burped, all at the same time, which she does when she's anxious. Her eyes got hard . . . as hard as eyes can get when you look like Reese Witherspoon. "That man walked out on us," she said for the hundredth time.

I took a slug of smoothie. Then I said the worst thing I could think of, which I'd been thinking for, like, forever. "He didn't walk out on me, Mom. I wasn't even born yet. He walked out on *you*. Just like everybody else."

I saw her flinch before I stormed into my room and slammed the door. I was sorry the minute the words came out of my mouth, but everything inside me felt incredibly screwed up.

I picked up my guitar. Making music was usually a way to take the edge off everything and make me feel better. But then I looked up and saw the framed picture of Kim and Max staring at me from my dresser. The photo was vintage '90s. Mom looked really young and really knocked up. She was balancing a sad little bouquet on her tummy, and Max, kind of grungy and wearing a tuxedo T-shirt, had his arm around her. They were both smiling, but anyone looking at them could tell they definitely were not going to be one of those couples who stayed married for sixty years and were so in love that they died within an hour of each other.

I took a pillow off my bed and threw it at them. The frame plunked down backward on the dresser.

Then I played around with my new song, "A Rock and a Sad Place" for about twenty minutes, trying to find the perfect groove until there was a feeble knock on the door.

A yellow paper slid under my bedroom door. I walked over and picked up a page from the *St. Louis Yellow Pages*. There was a huge ad for The Palace of The Plasma Prince and the words "Max's work" written on it and circled in red.

The crappy thing I said had hit home. Max was back. I didn't know when he came back, but I now knew he was here in St. Louis and where I could find him. My heart was beating so fast and so loud, it felt as if it was going to explode out of my chest. I thought I was going be one of the youngest people ever to have a heart attack, but I didn't have time for that.

I was finally going to meet my dad.

chapter two

I took the bus to Page Avenue, walked two blocks, and there it was: The Palace of The Plasma Prince, a gigantic TV superstore all decked out to look like a castle in Disneyland. I was getting a bad feeling in my stomach.

Next to the entrance was a life-sized cardboard cutout of the "prince" in a robe, tights, and a crown. He looked just like my photograph of Max if Max had aged sixteen years and morphed into Henry VIII. The bad feeling got worse.

Customers wandered the aisles, checking out the TV shows blasting from each set, while sales people wearing silly medieval vests and hats stalked them, waiting for the right moment to move in.

Then I saw him. He looked just like the cutout. He was pitching a very large screen TV to a couple who were fixated on *Judge Judy* while their toddler ran around hitting buttons on the other sets, causing blizzards of snow.

I watched from a few steps away as Max picked up the kid and let the monster child pull down Max's crown over his nose. I could tell that it hurt, but Max laughed a phony laugh and asked the couple if they wanted to review some payment plans.

"Thanks, but I don't think so," said the husband. "That was our landlord on *Judge Judy.* We just wanted to see him lose on a big screen." Max clicked off the TV with his scepter remote as they picked up the kid and headed toward the door.

I walked up to him. "Max Lambert?" I asked.

"The prince himself." He straightened his crown and pasted on the most bogus smile in smile history. "Picking out a plasma before you bring in Daddy with the credit card?"

"Oh no," I said. "My dad's already here."

"And I'll bet he wants the best for his little girl."

"You tell me," I said as my heart began pounding like a Black Sabbath bass line.

A puzzled Henry VIII looked down at me.

"I'm Katherine Lambert, your daughter."

"Holy Crappoly," he said.

That's what he said. I couldn't believe he was saying that after being a no-show in his daughter's life for sixteen years. I felt as if he had stabbed me in the heart with his stupid scepter remote but I didn't show it. I willed myself not to cry because I wasn't going to give him the satisfaction of knowing that he could hurt me.

"What did Kim tell you about me?"

"She told me you were my dad and you moved away for a long time. I've had a picture of you and my mom next to my bed my whole life."

"Damn her! She tell you how to find me?"

"You know this isn't exactly the welcome I was hoping for," I said, deadpan.

"I don't want to talk here," he whispered. "We better go back to my office."

"I hope there are no moats involved," I whispered back. "I'm not a very strong swimmer." He didn't even smile. Father or no father, Max was turning out to be a cheesy a-hole, and to top it off, he had no sense of humor.

He turned on his heel and motioned for me to follow him as he strode to the back of the store to a door marked THE GREAT HALL. When he opened the door, it looked more like THE GREAT CLOSET. There was a desk, a throne chair behind it, and another chair in front of it. On the desk was a half full bottle of Maker's Mark. He poured himself a goblet full and motioned for me to sit down.

"So she didn't tell you?"

"Tell me what?"

"I never moved away," he said. "And I'm not your dad."

Suddenly I couldn't breathe. I felt like I was going to pass out right then and there in the Great Closet.

"Wa-wa-what do you mean?" I stuttered. I had never stuttered before in my life.

Max took a gulp from his goblet and put his crown on the desk. "We were young and broke. I had a very rich grampa with a very big tumor, but if I wanted to inherit a dime, I had to have a kid. Gramps wanted to be sure his stingy genes were going to be passed down to another generation. Trouble was, I'd had the mumps, and I had no swimmers."

The room was kind of spinning, but I couldn't help but think that maybe that's why he didn't laugh at the moat joke—swimming was a sensitive subject.

"Well," he continued, taking another gulp, "Kim and I weren't getting along all that great, but she wanted a kid desperately, so she went to a sperm bank. I thought we were in the clear, but Gramps didn't trust me. He told me that when the baby was born he wanted a DNA test, so . . ."

"So you walked out on my pregnant mom and thought it was okay?"

Max had the decency to squirm a little bit. "I would have made a lousy father. She had a job, and she wanted you. It was the right call. She has you, and I have this." He gestured toward the store with his scepter remote.

I leaned over the desk, and even though I wanted to shout, somehow the words came out very quietly: "You have a cheesy store where you dress like the Prince of Pudge in wrinkled tights that probably give you a rash."

"Listen, kiddo," he said, "I have a kingdom." Then he actually winked at me. "Just between you and me, your mom still a hottie?"

I grabbed the scepter remote out of his hand and charged out the door. Running down the aisle, scrunching back the tears, I punched the remote so that every set I passed freaked out. When I got outside, I tossed the stupid thing into the nearest garbage can along with every single Max fantasy I may have had.

I hated him for what he did to me and to Kim. I hated Kim for not telling me the whole story. I was really glad that I wasn't related to him, but what I hated the most was that now, I had no father at all.

chapter three

When I confronted my mom, I thought that she would look at me with her sad, victimy look, but she actually didn't. Even though her eyes got a little misty, she knew what was coming, and I could tell she was prepared.

"He had to tell you, Katie. I couldn't," she said calmly.

"Why not?"

"I thought that you needed to look in the mirror and see a whole reflection, not just half. I thought that you needed a picture of your father in your heart even if he wasn't in your life. I thought . . ."

"You thought wrong!" I snapped. "You lied to me. You let me think I was someone I wasn't."

"You're right," she said. "As you got older, I knew I was making a big mistake. I kept planning to tell you, but I just never could, so I told myself it didn't matter. I think they call that 'denial.' The truth is, I didn't know what to do, and I was scared. I was scared you'd be hurt again, so I told myself I was protecting you."

"Didn't you know this day would come?" I asked.

"I kept pretending that it wouldn't. I'm so, so sorry."

Her eyes misted up again, but I knew if I started sympathizing, I was going to cry, and I hate crying. I hate being wimpy like my mom, who cries every time she hears anybody sing "How Am I Supposed to Live Without You," one of the most codependent songs of all time. I was going to be stronger than that, so I hardened my heart. I had stuff I needed to know.

"Did you think I would want that man for a father? He's a complete jerk."

"He wasn't when I married him," Kim said a little defensively. "He was artistic and a little eccentric, but he wanted to be an actor, and he was talented. He played the Duke of Buckingham in a regional production of *Henry VIII* and got very good reviews."

"*Oh wow*, good reviews in a regional production of one play. Here's the update: He can't let it go. He's playing Henry now, or maybe you know that. C'mon, tell me, Kim, who *is* my real father?"

"Your biological father was a sperm donor with a wonderful profile, honey." She was chattering now, just relieved that we were moving on. "He went to Harvard, he had more than one degree, and he was very musical. That's probably where you got your talent."

"Just tell me which sperm bank you used and what his number was," I cut in.

"He was a 'do not contact' donor. Most of them were back then. It doesn't matter, Katie."

"It does matter. It matters to me, Kim. I have a right to know who I am, no matter what kind of donor he was."

She hesitated. I could see that her mind was racing. "I don't want you to get hurt again." She had big tears in her eyes now.

"Don't you think it hurts not to know? You have lied to me my whole life, and it wasn't a little lie. It was the biggest lie ever. Every day that photo sat next to my bed, you were lying. Every time I looked at it and thought I was looking at my father, you were lying. If that matters to you even a little bit, then start telling me the truth. Help me find out who I am. Tell me which sperm bank you used and what his number was. Please, please don't make me hate you. You owe it to me, Mom. You know you do."

At that moment, I saw something click. I think that was the moment when she got where I was coming from. I'll give her one thing: my mom was big on understanding. She pulled out one of her pink notecards and wrote "806, Cryosperm Bank" on it.

"I love you," she said, handing it to me. "I wanted you very much. I thought that would be enough."

"But it wasn't and now you know that," I said.

"I do, I really do," my mom whispered, kind of choked

up. "I have to leave for work in five. I'll have my cell phone turned on."

I threw an "I know" over my shoulder and dove into my room. "Call me if you want to talk," Kim yelled after me.

I sat staring at the card for at least five minutes as if my dad's face would somehow appear on it. It was all I had of him, my father, 806, the other half of me.

Slowly, a memory came creeping into my brain. It must have been a year ago. I was getting dressed for school while watching *The Today Show,* and this dude came on who was a sperm donor. He was interviewed with some of the kids he had fathered who had found him. He was handsome and smart and so glad his kids had gotten in touch with him. He loved them, they loved him, and the kids all loved each other. They were like some kind of spermy *Brady Bunch.*

Then this woman came on the show who ran a website where donor kids could find each other and maybe even find their donor dads. I couldn't remember the name of it, but I pulled out my laptop and googled "sperm donor children" and that's how I found your organization, www.donorsiblingcontact.org. I read about the way it worked at least a hundred times, and even though it had sibling in the name, there were a whole bunch of dads listed who were looking for their kids. I guess not everyone had a "do not contact" father. Just lucky me!

My only gripe with you, DSC.org, was that I had to swipe my mom's credit card to register and then slip it back into her wallet. It was so easy for me, I wondered if maybe my real father was some kind of thief or scam artist, and it was in my blood.

I know my mom probably would have given it to me, but I didn't want to have another conversation with her that day. I figured we'd have the conversation when she got her credit card bill, and maybe by then I'd have some half brothers and sisters backing me up. I also figured if she didn't know what I was doing, she couldn't come up with one of her lists of reasons not to do it. Now I'm not a socialist or anything, but I think you guys should let kids post for free instead of turning them into credit card thieves, but I guess you need money to run the site.

Anyway, I want to tell whoever's running things that, in my opinion, you have a pretty good system. I looked up Cryosperm, St. Louis, and the number 806 wasn't there so I posted it with my email address. When I saw my entry on the screen, I got a little flash of happiness like something sweet was going to happen. I started thinking about who my father really was and wondering what kind of music he liked. I wondered if he could be an actual musician, if he'd like my songs, and how we'd feel about each other if we ever met. Then I picked up my guitar, wrote a song called "Finding Me," and waited for my brothers or sisters or "do not contact" father to email me.

chapter four

I checked in online at Donor Sibling Contact at least twice every day, even though I knew I would be getting an email if my donor sibs or donor dad saw my posting. It just made me feel good to see the number 806 out there in cyberspace. I didn't tell anyone, even Sasha, about your website, but I did tell her about Max not being my father and being a donor spawn and all. She said "oh my god" in all the right spots and mentioned that, oddly enough, even after all that bad stuff, I seemed to be in a better mood. I didn't tell her why: which was that my biological father didn't even know I existed, not that he didn't care. Now I had a real hope I was going to find the rest of me. That felt really good.

Two weeks after I joined DSC.org, I went to band rehearsal at Sasha's. I didn't know why I called it "rehearsal." It wasn't like we were going to perform anywhere, but "practice" sounded so amateur. Sasha's dad always moved out the cars and let us use their garage whenever we got together to rehearse.

Sasha and I first met at the school talent contest at the beginning of freshman year when she played percussion and sang "In the Long Run." I'm not exactly the chatty type—I hardly ever talk to people I don't know—but I was compelled to go up to her at intermission and tell her that I was a fan of "old guy" rock groups like The Eagles and that her version of the song was a giant step beyond awesome. She then told me that she thought my guitar and vocal performance of The Band's "I Shall Be Released" was so fantabulous it almost made her cry.

Before we even thought about it, we were babbling about music like besties because neither of us was really into what we were hearing on top-ten radio. It was kind of crazy, but we both loved the old, old, old classics. We couldn't stop talking, and by the end of the show, we had decided to form a band. All we needed was a great bass player, and Sasha said she had the perfect one, someone who she'd known since they were little kids because their moms were BFFs.

That dude turned out to be Dylan Stewart, who actually was a very good, serious musician. Unfortunately, he segued from saying "hello" to becoming nuts about me, and sadly I was not interested.

My noninterest, however, didn't affect Dylan in the slightest. He got increasingly "shmoopy" until he reminded me of my mom, who was the scary poster child for misplaced emotion. I sometimes thought he was really off his rocker, like he had a major leak in his think tank. He once told me I was the coolest, most talented human being on the planet, which made me excruciatingly uncomfortable. The way his eyes got all soft when he looked at me seemed to push all my snippy buttons.

When I got to Sasha's, Dylan was waiting for me.

"Hey Dylan," I said without much enthusiasm.

He jumped up and ran to meet me. "Hey, KT, let me take your guitar or your laptop or something."

"Jesus, Dylan, they don't have carry-on restrictions here. In case you haven't noticed, I brought it this far. It's fine. I'm *fine.*"

"I'll be down in a minute," Sasha yelled from inside the house.

I turned on my computer in case I got any emails and began tuning my guitar. Dylan hovered like I was a light bulb and he was a flying bug. "I wrote a new song," he said. "It's called 'Please Want Me.'"

I sighed. "Please tell me it's not about me," I said. "And please quit writing songs about me. It's embarrassing. I'm embarrassed already, and I haven't even heard it."

"You're my muse, KT," he answered, his big brown eyes all gleamy and disgustingly sincere. "I think about you and words pour into my brain and music pours out of my fingers."

"If I knew what that meant, I could argue with you, but I don't. I like you, Dylan, but not in the same way. Please, please try to get over me, like, now."

"Your computer battery is low," he said. "You better plug in."

"And why are you carrying your laptop everywhere all of a sudden?" chimed in Sasha as she walked into the garage. She really knows me and smelled something was weird, so I broke down and told her and Dylan everything. The truth is, I was dying to share it with somebody and they were the most likely (and possibly the only) candidates.

"It would be sweet if you found someone like a sister to talk to," Dylan said.

"If you're looking for a bitchy sister," Sasha offered, "I'd be happy to give you mine."

I laughed, but Dylan was right. I'd dreamed about having sibs almost as much as finding my donor dad, but I just said "whatever." Then Sasha took off her jacket and I freaked out. Sasha had a tattoo. There on her forearm was a big, beautiful snake. I had wanted to get a tattoo desperately and had even talked Mom into it. She said yes if she could go with me and it was a tiny, tasteful one. But Sasha's parents had said "absolutely not." They were Jewish, and if you've got a tattoo, you can't get buried in a Jewish cemetery. So I agreed I wouldn't do it because she couldn't, and here she had gone and become "the tattooed serpent queen" without telling me before or after. I felt totally betrayed. I couldn't believe that Sasha would let me down. Not her, too. Not my best and only friend.

"Why are you getting all red?" Sasha asked me.

"A snake is a really appropriate tat," I hissed. "I was the one who thought of getting a tat, remember, but I opted out based on loyalty to you. I'm working hard to be a real artist, and that means I have to stay in touch with my dark side."

"You *are* dark, KT, and you *are* an artist. You don't need a tat to prove it," Dylan declared.

"Just shut up, Dylan!" I snapped. "I'm talking to Miss Sneaky Snake here."

"The pain was excruciating," said Sasha, rolling her eyes in agony. "You would have loved it. You could have called up the anguish for a song."

"That's what I mean. My life is my inspiration, and you know it. So did your parents convert or something? How could you? Why didn't you tell me?"

Sasha burst out laughing. "Calm down, oh Pissed Off One," she cackled. She was laughing so hard she snorted when she talked. "It's a temp. It washes off." Then she tapped me on the head with her drumstick and hit the snare and cymbal for punctuation.

I was so mortified I didn't know what to do. "Just kidding," I muttered. "I knew that. I was putting you on. Now let's get going."

Dylan looked relieved, Sasha seemed to buy it, and I felt kind of guilty for snapping at him, so I taught them "A Rock and a Sad Place." Dylan came up with some bass lines and backgrounds that were very cool. We rehearsed for about two hours and then we started packing up. Just when I was wondering if we were good enough to play Kroeger's Koffee House at Saturday night open call, my computer started shouting "You've Got Mail." My heart thumped every time I got an email alert. I didn't want to show how excited I was, though, so I put my guitar in its case really slowly.

"Aren't you going to check your email?" asked Sasha.

"Oh," I said, pretending I hadn't noticed, "I guess so."

They both peered over my shoulders as I clicked open my mailbox. There were two new messages. One must have come while we were playing too loudly to hear it. The first, sent an hour ago, was from Swimmy@Yahoo.com with the subject line "806 kid"; and the other, just sent, was from abracadabra@pobox.net, and it read, "Good chance we're sibs." I was paralyzed. Their emails said that they'd decided we should all meet at Fuddruckers tomorrow at noon wearing something that said "806" on it. Would have been nice if they had asked my opinion but . . .

"Don't go in there all bent out of shape, KT," Dylan warned me. "Show them your good side."

"I didn't know I had one," I said.

"You do. Remember when we were playing at talent day last year and I forgot my part? You covered for me and didn't even yell at me."

"You only forgot two measures. It was no big deal."

"Yes, it was. That's when I knew we were meant to be together."

"But we're not, Dylan. I don't want to be with anyone. I

have seen with my own eyes that being with someone never works out. I know that for a fact, believe me."

"What I believe is, one day you'll change your mind, and I'll still be here," he said firmly. "You gotta believe, KT. You never know what amazing things can happen."

"Yeah, amazingly bad," I retorted.

Dylan sighed. "Now are you gonna answer them?"

I had so many emotions running through me that my hands were shaking, but I managed to send both of them an answer from Nonameband@aol.com. It just said, "See you tomorrow."

"You have to tell me everything immediately after you meet them," Sasha ordered. "Do not breathe more than five times before texting me every word that was said."

"Call me when you're ready to talk," said Dylan, looking deep into my eyes. "Are you okay?"

"I'm good," I said. But I wasn't. I was scared and a little sick to my stomach because I had a feeling that tomorrow my whole life was going to change, and then I realized something else. I didn't know if Swimmy and Abracadabra were male or female. So right then I started hoping that at least one of them was a girl. Dylan was right, I really did want a sister. It would be sweet if she was vegetarian and liked the music I liked. Maybe she'd even have a real tattoo. Most of all, maybe she'd be someone I could count on.

chapter five

I got to Fuddruckers at ten minutes before noon, grabbed a table in the back, and stuck a sign on my guitar case with 806 written on it. I sat the case straight up on the chair next to me, ordered a salad, and waited for Swimmy and Abracadabra.

While I was cooling my heels, it suddenly dawned on me that there was a chance I could know my sibs, at least by sight. I had looked up Cryosperm on the Internet, and back when Kim was sperm hunting, they were the only sperm bank in the greater St. Louis area. Central High was huge, and a whole lot of middle schools from all over the city fed into it. I tried to remember if I'd seen anyone at school who looked at all like me.

Then I got a flash. It seemed to me that Amanda Cooley, editor of the paper and one of the truly hip, kind of resembled me on my very best days. She could possibly be walking into Fuddruckers any minute. I would be so stoked to be related to someone like her.

My eyes were glued to the door, and my heart raced anytime someone my age walked in. By twelve fifteen, it felt as if I had been there for hours. I had given myself a headache from staring at the entrance, so I was more ticked off than nervous when I heard a loud sneeze and looked up.

"Oh shit!" came out of me before I could stop it.

Standing in front of me was Gabe Butcherelli, a bookwormy nerd who was in the science club. He wasn't the cool kind of nerd who was funny and brilliant. He was the nerd everyone felt sorry for, who did bad magic tricks at the last school talent show. He was skinny, wore thick glasses, had mousy brown hair, was always coughing or sneezing, and he didn't look anything like me. To make things worse, he was wearing a Breathe-Rite strip across his nose that had "806" written on it. It was beyond human comprehension that Butcherelli and I could be related. And then it got worse.

As he blew his nerdy nose and sat down, I heard a voice say, "Sorry I'm late, I've got a messed-up sense of direction. I got kind of lost."

I looked up to see a nightmare from the opposite end of the high school food chain. There stood Jesse Worthington-Flax: captain of the swim team, blond golden boy, dumb jock, "Mr. Perfect," major heart-throb, and major a-hole. He had an "806" sticky note stuck to his varsity jacket. A large group of girls in school, with the notable exception of me and Sasha, had the hots for him, but Sash and I couldn't stand him and his posse of mentally challenged sports fanatics.

He took in the sorry sight of me and the nerd and tried to smile, but even he couldn't manage to pull that off. He just sat down, stunned, and we all stared at each other for what felt like forever. The disappointment in the air was stronger than the smell of dead cow burgers.

"This is obviously a shock and a disappointment to all of us," I finally said. "Clearly we are not each other's people, and neither of you is the sister I was hoping for, but maybe we should swap bios while we're here?"

"Yeah," Jesse said. "I'm hungry."

After he ordered a hamburger with extra bacon and Abracadabra ordered chicken soup (because, he explained, it sometimes cleared his nose), I wanted to disown the two of them on the spot and get out of Fuddruckers right then and there. Anyone who ate the meat of helpless dead animals was a project to work on, like Sasha. But Sasha was worth the effort. This jock was not.

These nightmare sibs couldn't have been less like me, but I'd agreed to fill them in on my story. I told them the screwy saga of my life with Mom up to now and all about Max and the big lie. I neglected to mention, however, that just looking at them made me feel really bad about the genes we shared.

"My parents lied to me, too," said Gabe, slurping away. "But I'm not mad at them. My dad was like Max. No swimmers. He felt really ashamed about that, and he's always wanted kids. So my mom got inseminated, and they didn't tell anyone, not even me."

"How'd you find out?" Jesse asked, chomping on his burger in the most revolting way possible.

"We did blood typing in science class, and I got my parents' blood types off their organ donor cards. They were both O, and I turned out to be A, so I had to have had an A parent."

"Did they freak when you told them you knew?" I asked.

"Not really. First, I thought my mom had cheated on my dad, so I was really relieved to find out it wasn't that. And they were so sad and guilty about not telling me the truth that I felt sorry for them. My mom's the best. My dad's a real tough kind of guy, but he loves me for me. He's interested in everything I do, even if he doesn't totally get it."

"If things are so perfect at the old homestead, then why did you want to follow your '806' connection?" I wondered if I'd be searching for my dad if I had a great one at home.

"I'm curious about my donor dad. Not what he looks like, 'cause I look just like my mom—same face, same bad eyes—but I wonder if he's smart and if he likes magic and if he's allergic to everything that grows, the way I am. I've always wanted some answers to a bunch of question marks in my life."

There was another long silence. "My turn," said Jesse, after ordering another side of bacon. "I've always known I was a donor kid because I have two moms."

"That is beyond cool," I said. "I've always considered lesbians to be the ultimate individualists." This made me see Mr. Perfect in a new and cooler light.

"I guess so," Jesse answered. "It wasn't always like that, though. I got teased about it in elementary school. Some of my teachers even acted weird, but Liz and Tina have always helped me deal with the crap. I just can't handle the latest."

"What's the latest?" the nerd and I asked in unison.

"They're breaking up. Now we're gonna be screwed up and split up like almost everyone I know. They work together as party planners and after their next job, Tina's moving back to Boston where she's from, and Liz is staying here. They told me it's up to me to decide who I want to live with by August, and I can't do that. Tina's my biological mom, but I love Liz, too, and I don't want to change schools and all that. I have to choose between them, and I can't. When they asked me what they could do to make it easier, I made them give me my donor dad's number."

"Did one of them go straight?" It just popped out. I seem to have no edit mechanism.

"Uh-uh. I asked that." Jesse shook his head. "They're both still gay. They said they don't feel the way they used to, that they've lost what they used to have, and they need to be apart. I gotta find my dad so maybe I can live with him, or if I tell them that's gonna happen, maybe they'll stay together and try harder."

"Using 806 as a weapon may not be happening for you, Swimmy," I told him. "He was a 'do not contact' donor. That means he wanted to be anonymous and probably still does."

I guessed Tina and Liz hadn't shared that little tidbit because for a moment his face crumpled, and he didn't look all that perfect. Then he ordered another bacon burger and went off somewhere in his head.

"Hey, wanna see a magic trick?" Gabe offered. "This is called 'Silver Smoke'." Without waiting for an answer, he stood up and did some lame trick that made quarters disappear into smoke.

"Wanna see it again?" he asked as a couple at the next table flailed their arms to wave the smoke away.

"How could we have the same father?" I meant to say it in my head, but it came out of my mouth.

"Beats me," said Jesse, looking at me with bacon grease lining the corner of his mouth.

"Bacon burgers make me sick," I told him. "I hate that my mom works at Burger Boy. I'm a vegetarian."

"You look like one," he said.

"What does that mean?" I asked, although I thought I knew. "What do you think it means?" he asked.

I ignored the question, although I knew it meant I looked like an oddball.

"Do either of you have a webbed toe or two?" Gabe

blurted out. I think he was trying to head off whatever was coming between Swimmy and me.

"No," we both answered. "Do you?'

"Of course not," he retorted.

"Then why did you ask?" I wanted to know.

"I don't know. Just in case," he muttered.

"In case of what?" Jesse asked.

"This is getting too weird," I said, standing up and picking up my guitar case.

"You play guitar?" Jesse was full of brilliant questions.

"No," I said, "I just carry around a case."

"Talk about weird," Gabe commented.

I couldn't listen to them or look at them for another minute. My sibling dream had crashed when I saw them, and now it was going up in flames.

I threw "Have a nice life" over my shoulder as I headed for the door. I never, ever, *ever* wanted to see those two again. I was aching inside. They didn't know it, and I knew deep down they couldn't help it, but they had broken my heart just by being who they were.

chapter six

I didn't know what to do with myself. I didn't feel like texting Sasha or calling Dylan. I just wanted to forget the Fuddruckers nightmare, so I wandered over to Forest Park, sat on the grass, and noodled on my guitar. I wanted to get lost in my music, and I guess I did because when I looked at my watch, it was almost six. I hightailed it home, hoping I'd be able to get into my room before my mom got back from work. I had told her I was meeting them, and I knew she would be full of questions I didn't want to answer. But no such luck. There she was waiting for me, all excited.

"What were they like?" she wanted to know. She was already glowing with the happy news she hadn't gotten yet.

"Like people I never want to see again," I snapped.

Her face fell. "What do you mean?"

"My brothers are Jesse Worthington-Flax, an idiot jock, and Gabe Butcherelli, a nerd with allergy problems. I've seen both of them in school. I have zero in common with them, so I'm not really seeing family there. I don't want to talk about it anymore."

I caught a glimpse of her shocked, sad expression before I slammed into my room. I was thankful she knew me well enough not to follow me, even though she wanted to try and make it better. There was no way to make this better.

I lay down on my bed to relive the horror of it all, and I guess I dozed off because I woke up to hear my computer yelling "mail truck." I figured it was Sasha or Dylan and wanted to put off rehashing what had happened, so I lay there for a while thinking about how just when you think everything is the total pits, it can get even worse.

When I finally made it over to my computer, I couldn't believe what I was seeing. I slammed my hand over my mouth so I wouldn't scream as my stomach clenched and churned.

There was an email and the subject was: TO MY CHILDREN FROM THEIR BIRTH FATHER, DONOR 806. I opened it and saw it was addressed to "Swimmy" and "Abracadabra" as well. For a minute I couldn't breathe from excitement, and then fear took over. I was scared to open it. Scared of who he would be and if he'd be the biggest disappointment of my life after Jesse and Gabe.

I'm not religious, but I whispered a prayer, "Please God,

don't let him be a creep," and then I clicked "Read."

"My dear children," the email read. "First let me say that I was overjoyed to see your postings. I have long regretted my decision, seventeen years ago, to be a 'do not contact' donor, but it was only today that I discovered this website. At the time I made the decision to be a donor, I had no idea of the import of what I was doing. I hope I can make that up to you.

"Let me tell you a little about myself. I grew up in St. Louis and played varsity soccer at St. Louis University. I met my beloved wife when we were both med students at Harvard. We share a practice, but most of our time is devoted to Doctors Without Borders. We have only recently returned from Zimbabwe, where we ran a mobile medical clinic.

"A family is the river of life and you, my children, are examples of a miraculous faith in its loving power. I can't wait to meet you all. Dr. Jeffrey Rosenberg."

I must have read it fifty times. Oh my god! He was so cool. Harvard! Zimbabwe! A man dedicated to serving others. The absolute opposite of Henry VIII. He was everything I could ever hope for, and he wanted a relationship. Unfortunately, that relationship included my puke-worthy brothers, but that was the least of it. I was going to have a dad!

We exchanged emails, and Doctor Dad sent us his address in Ladue, a fancy suburb, and invited us to visit the next day. I agreed to take the bus with my lame sibs since it made sense for us to get there together. Jesse was really stoked. His plan to scare his moms into staying together might have a shot now.

Just then my cell phone rang. It was Dylan.

"I was worried when I didn't hear from you," he said. "I thought you might have been kidnapped or something."

"I just wasn't ready to talk."

"Are you ready now?"

"You bet your best bass riff I am."

"You sound really up. Were your sibs cool? Do you have a sister?"

"No and no. My sibs are Gabe Butcherelli and Jesse Worthington-Flax."

There was dead silence on the other end of the phone.

"You didn't hurt them, did you?"

"No, I left before that could happen."

"So why do you sound so good?"

"Because we all just got an email from our 'do not contact' father who changed his mind and wants to meet us tomorrow."

Dylan actually sounded a little choked up. "You see, good stuff can happen to you even though I know you don't think it can."

"Historically it hasn't, so I base my expectations on that. It makes sense to me."

"Things are always changing, KT, except for one. I'm always here," he said.

"Until you're not," I answered. "I gotta go now," I said and hung up the phone. There was nothing else to say, and I wanted to enjoy the good feeling I was feeling.

And then I realized something that made me even happier. It was a really, really good thing I hadn't gotten that tattoo because I was going to be a Rosenberg.

⁂

We didn't even sit together on the almost empty bus. Jesse stretched out on the back seat and went to sleep with his head on an overnight bag that had a soccer ball tied to it. Guess he thought he and the old man would kick it around together. Gabe stuck his stuffed nose in a book called *The Science of Magic,* and I sat across the aisle reading a paperback titled *Every Goy's Guide to Jewish Expressions.* My mom had bought the book before she went on JDate. Like her, I wanted to be totally prepared and had already thought about converting. I pictured how happy my dad would be when I told him. I had seen videos of Sasha's bat mitzvah when she was thirteen, and it was very cool. I wondered if I could have a belated one at my age.

The doctor's house was beautiful, a perfect family home. It had a cute little path with flowers on either side leading up to the front door. We stood in front of it on the sidewalk, just staring. Then Jesse took a preppy sweater out of his bag and slipped it on. He looked like a Ralph Lauren ad in one of Mom's fashion magazines. I shot him a look.

"What?" he asked. "I want to look like I fit in. I could be living here."

I rolled my eyes, and we walked up to the front door. I went to ring the bell, but Gabe stopped me.

"Wait," he snorted and pasted a Breathe-Rite strip over his nose. "I want to be clear, nasally."

"That is disgusting," I said, ripping it off his nose. "Which one of you is more annoying?"

"Probably me," said Gabe as I rang the doorbell. We held our collective breath, and then the door opened.

There stood a beaming Dr. Jeffrey Rosenberg. He wore horn-rimmed glasses and looked as if he were in his late thirties.

He was about 5'10", lean and good-looking, with a warm smile and nice twinkly eyes. He was wearing one of those sweaters with patches on the elbows. He looked smart and kind and understanding.

He was the perfect dad and . . . he was African American. Yes, he was African American. His skin was a warm beige, like the color of Dave (Pink Floyd) Gilmour's Stratocaster, but he was African American beyond a doubt. Next to him stood his pretty, Michelle Obamaish, pregnant wife surrounded by their kids: two teens who were younger than we were and a set of twins about nine. All of our smiles faded as everyone stared at each other for a long time. Then we introduced ourselves.

"Your mothers must have very powerful genes," the doctor said finally. "Please come in."

The kids surrounded us as we entered. The twins were smiling and curious, and the older ones looked suspicious and pissed off. I didn't blame them. Who would want to share their perfect dad with three strangers?

"KT, Gabe, and Jesse, I'd like you to meet my family," said Doctor Rosenberg. "My wife Nicole, my little ones Rashida and Kidada, my daughter Susan, and my eldest, Marcus."

Mrs. Doctor Rosenberg forced a smile, the little girls giggled, Susan scowled and nodded, and Marcus just stood there, looking cool in a surfer T under a bright blue shirt, emitting waves of hostility.

"Let's go into the den," suggested Mrs. Doctor. "You can join us later," she told the kids as we made our way down an elegant book-lined hallway.

It was then that Gabe whispered, a little too loudly, "This is so crazy wonderful! We're biracial. I'm finally gonna be cool."

"Shhh!" I hissed. "Don't get ahead of yourself."

The Rosenbergs led us into a beautiful wood-paneled den and gestured for us to sit on a cushy couch. The walls were lined with all sorts of diplomas and awards. We couldn't stop staring at the Rosenbergs, and they couldn't stop staring at us. It was more than a little uncomfortable. Finally Dr. Jeffrey spoke.

"Being adopted myself, I know how important it is to connect with biological family," he told us. "My late adoptive parents, Susan and Marcus Rosenberg, were extraordinary people, and we loved each other very much, but I've always been curious about my birthparents. I'm still trying to locate them."

"You're sure your number was 806?" I said, just because someone had to.

"Absolutely, I have a certificate," he responded. He opened his desk drawer and whipped out one that thanked Donor 806 for his donation.

"Oh, I see," I answered brilliantly. The silence was deafening.

Mrs. Doctor picked up a silver tray with little square doughy things on it and offered it to Jesse. "Would you like a knish?"

"Only if you've got some ketchup," Swimmy answered.

The Rosenbergs chuckled like it was a joke. I'd been at Sasha's house enough to know that knishes and ketchup didn't go together, so I kicked him under the coffee table and changed the subject. "Dr. Rosenberg, my mom told me that your profile said you played some musical instruments."

"Yes," he said. "I tickled the ivories in my youth."

"I'm in a band and I write songs," I said a little shyly. "I play guitar. Would you play something for me?"

"I haven't touched a keyboard in years, but I became proficient on the didgeridoo while working with the aborigines in Australia. Would you like to hear one of my favorites?"

"It would give me..." I ran through my *Goy's Guide* in my head, mentally searching for just the right word. *"Naches,"* I told him. That meant it would give me pleasure.

He walked to the corner of the room, picked up a skinny leather case, and pulled out a long, painted, wooden instrument. Then he sat cross-legged on the floor. "This is called 'The Kangaroo Hop,'" he said, putting it to his lips.

"It goes on for a while," Mrs. Doctor sighed.

He blew into it, and this really spooky sound came out and went on and on and on for about five minutes. When he stopped, we all applauded.

"Wow!" I said, trying to muster enthusiasm. "That must be really hard to play."

The doc smiled and put his didge away. I thought I saw the wife raise her eyes to the ceiling as if in thanks as he turned his attention to Jesse.

"Just looking at you, Jesse, I would say you're an athlete. Do you play soccer?"

"Actually, no. I'm a varsity swimmer," Jesse responded.

"Ah," said Dr. Rosenberg, in order to say something. "What do you excel in at school? What are your academic interests?"

Silence descended again for a full beat. Jesse was stumped. He had to make a choice whether to tell the disappointing truth or make stuff up. He went with the truth.

"I kind of haven't figured that out yet," he answered, looking at the floor. "But I'm working on it."

I wanted to do something to rescue poor Swimmy, but I couldn't figure out what. It was Gabe who saved the day.

He leaned forward and made real eye contact. "Dr. Rosenberg, may I ask you something personal?"

"Anything at all, Gabe."

"Do you have any allergies?"

"Not a one. You can roll me in ragweed, I don't even sniffle," he replied. Then he looked at Gabe intently. "Tell me, son, was your family open with you about using a donor?"

"No," the nerdy one answered, "I found out in a blood typing experiment in school. My folks are both O, and I'm type A, so they had to own up."

The Rosenbergs gasped and locked eyes. Then they both stood up.

"Unfortunately," the doctor said, "it seems that I'm not your father. I did have my doubts since we don't have any physical similarities, but now I know for sure."

He opened the same desk drawer and pulled out another certificate. It was from The American Red Cross and read: "TO DOCTOR JEFFREY ROSENBERG WITH GRATITUDE FOR THE MANY LIVES

YOU HAVE SAVED WITH YOUR GENEROUS DONATIONS OF BLOOD." At the bottom in tiny print was the note: "Your type O blood is known as the universal donor."

Gabe, Jesse, and I all got up from the cushy couch at the same time as if we were connected.

"I'm so, so sorry. I'm afraid this must be some sort of tragic logistical error," Dr. Rosenberg declared with a sincere look of sympathy.

"Or a very sick practical joke," his wife mused suspiciously.

"I'd stick with 'tragic logistical error,'" I told them, trying not to lose it. "Believe me, it's not any kind of joke. We thought we were going to find our biological father. It's what we all dreamed about, what we all wanted more than anything."

"I don't understand how this mix-up could have happened," the doc said sincerely. "I'm so terribly sorry."

The dude looked almost as sad as we did while his wife had the expression of someone who has just dodged a bullet.

"I guess we better go," I said. I couldn't wait to get out of there.

We all walked to the front door, not knowing what to say.

"I sincerely hope you find your father," Doctor Rosenberg told us. He gave us each a heartfelt, backbreaking hug, and then we were standing outside as the door closed gently behind us.

"I couldn't have lived there anyway," Jesse muttered.

"And they were so close to asking you," I snapped.

"Well, I thought Susan was really pretty," he added, out of nowhere.

Just then the door opened, a bright blue arm shot out, and Jesse's overnight bag was deposited on the doorstep. The door slammed shut, then opened again, and his soccer ball came flying out. I scooted over to where it had landed, picked up the ball, and threw it at the door.

"Thank you, Marcus!" I shouted.

"He probably can't hear you. He's too busy doing a happy dance," Jesse said, picking up his stuff.

"He doesn't matter. Forget him," I whispered to Jesse.

"That's the closest I'll ever get to being cool," Gabe mused sadly.

"But you know," Jesse remarked, "it's weird that the doc gives away all that bodily fluid. Blood, sperm . . . does anyone need pee?"

"Why are you making jokes?" I asked, holding back the tears. "It's not funny that we have no dad. Don't you care?"

"I know it's not funny, and I care a lot," Jesse answered, his voice cracking a little.

"My dad says things happen for a reason," Gabe offered.

"I always hated that expression," I told him. "How could all our parents have gotten the number wrong?" I asked no one in particular.

"It's mathematically improbable that something like that would happen," said Gabe. "There's got to be another answer."

I was so fed up that I couldn't even talk. I pulled *Every Goy's Guide* out of my pocket and tossed it into the gutter. I'd been using my mom's pink notecard with "806" written on it as a bookmark, and it slipped out as the book hit the ground and flipped upside down. We all stared at it, and our mouths fell open.

"Oh my god!" I whispered.

"Damn!" said Jesse.

"Eureka!" Gabe snorted.

The card, upside down, now read 908.

chapter seven

Going home, we sat together on the bus, trying to make sense of what just happened. Someone must have mixed up the donor number. That was a given. We took turns trying to figure out how it had happened until we were almost at our stop. Then Gabe snorted some organic nose spray. It seemed to clear his brain so that he was able to hit on something that made sense.

"Back when our parents were looking for donors, Cryosperm was the only sperm bank in St. Louis. My mom told me that they looked through a big book that some nurse put together with all the donor profiles and numbers. What if one of the nurses was a little dyslexic and switched

806 and 908 next to the profiles? Our moms would have chosen 806, thinking they were choosing 908."

"Then why aren't we all beige?" I wanted to know.

"Because my mom told me that the donor number was at the top of the profile on the page and, embedded in the profile at the bottom, there was a security code number that you peeled off and showed them for the vial of sperm. So when you told the nurse who you wanted, you showed her the code number, which would have been the correct code for 908 even though 908 was listed as 806. Get it?"

"I think so," Jesse said. "That way if a wannabe mom was numerically challenged, they couldn't get the wrong sperm by reversing or inverting numbers. They had to get the sperm of the profile they wanted. Each of our moms picked the profile of 806 that should have been marked 908."

Not bad for a dumb jock, I thought.

"So, do you guys wanna post 908 on DSC.org and see if he contacts us?" asked Gabe.

"Hell no," said Jesse. "My situation is desperate. I can't wait for a 'no contact' to contact me."

"I'm on a roll," I told them. "I can't deactivate now. I say we get our bio dad's profile and we contact him. Maybe he's like our almost-dad. Maybe he's sorry he was a 'do not contact.'"

"How do we get his profile?" Jesse wanted to know.

"They probably keep all that info in their filing system," Gabe said. "Or maybe they've transferred it to a computer?"

"One of us should call and see if we can find out," I said.

They both looked at me as the bus pulled into our stop.

"Okay, I'll do it," I said, and then I uttered the words I thought I would never say. "Gimme your numbers, and I'll call you tonight."

We piled off the bus and went our separate ways, thinking our separate thoughts, and I called Sasha on my cell to fill her in while I walked home.

"I can't talk, K," she said. "My mom's working late, so my dad and I are on our way to pig out at McDonald's"

"No burgers, please, I'm begging you. Have a salad."

"You really are out to change the world one meal at a time, my *veggie* friend."

"Just work on your dad, will you?"

"Okay. You have my word—no meat. I promise to try to influence my dad, but tonight he's king because he's taking me to a . . . drum roll . . . Kings of Leon concert."

"How did you pull that off? I thought your dad hated rock concerts."

"I told him that sharing music is a father-daughter bonding experience."

"I wouldn't know, but have a great time," I told her. Then I hung up, feeling kind of ashamed of myself because I wasn't totally happy for her. I was really jealous that she had a dad to share a dinner and a concert with, and I was going home to an empty house.

When I got there, I did what I said I would. I called the sperm clinic and tried to sound like a customer. Then I called Swimmy, and he conferenced in Abracadabra.

"Here it is," I told them. "I found out zip. I think I sounded young or something. The Sperminator dude told me that if I was a real patient, I should come in person, and then I'd see how their files were kept. Then he hung up on me."

"Then that's what we'll have to do," said Jesse. "We gotta go to Cryosperm and figure out a way to get 908's information." And right then and there, we hatched a plan to take back our birthright.

⸸ ⸸ ⸸

The next day we met at Jesse's. He had a really nice house. There were sports trophies and pictures of him all over the place. The kitchen had two stoves and a humongous fridge that I'm sure had never had any Burger Boy stuff in it. On the counter was a framed cover of a magazine called *Catering Quarterly,* with a picture of his moms and the headline: "Liz Worthington and Tina Flax Share Success Secrets." It was perfect. I could totally see why Jesse was bummed out.

His moms had taken the car and told Jesse he could use their catering van if he had to go anywhere, so we piled in and headed for Cryosperm. We actually seemed to be getting along okay until I realized that I should have changed into my outfit at Jesse's house. I wanted to go back, but Jesse said it was too late, we were almost there. And if I was so smart, then why didn't I think of that before.

Then Gabe had a sneezing fit, ran out of tissues, and sprayed saliva all over the place. The two of them shifted back into their most annoying selves. I told them to just shut up, and that they'd have to get out when we arrived and let me change in the van. When we pulled into the lot, that's what they did.

When I slid back the door and stepped out in my candy striper's uniform (which I found stashed in the back of my mom's closet), Jesse fell off the skateboard he'd been fooling around with, and Gabe kind of gulped.

"You look very, uh, authentic," he said.

"If you weren't you, you'd be kind of hot," Jesse admitted.

"I try not to think anyone's hot, 'cause no one thinks I'm hot. But if I did ..." Gabe began.

"Yeah, yeah, yeah," I interrupted. "Whatever." And then it hit me. "You guys, this is where we were conceived. We're standing outside the building where our creation began."

"Yeah, this is where 908 did his thing, all by himself," Jesse whispered almost reverently.

"Ugh, I never thought of it that way!" I snapped. "And I don't want to."

"Don't forget the magazines I bought," Gabe reminded me, looking embarrassed.

"Let's do it, Jesse!" I ordered, taking the stack of girlie rags from Gabe and heading for the entrance with Jesse behind me.

When I peeked inside the door of Cryosperm, it looked kind of like a regular doctor's office. There was one of those high desks that the receptionist usually sits behind, and in back of it, a bunch of file cabinets.

No one was in the waiting room, and a sign with an arrow pointed down a hallway to the "Donor Rooms."

Suddenly, a dude in a pink shirt and lavender tie popped up behind the counter. He clicked on an intercom and bellowed, "Room Nine, are you making a donation or having a party with yourself?"

"I have a hand cramp," Room Nine whined.

"Boo-hoo," said the dude. "Man up and deliver. I'm going to need the room in five minutes . . . no pressure."

A donor walked up to the desk carrying a labeled cup and put it down. "Can I keep this, Lowell?" he asked, holding up a copy of *Lusty Latinas* magazine. Lowell snatched it out of his hand, and the guy flew past me out the front door. Seems like everyone was afraid of Lowell. But I wasn't. I was on a mission.

I signaled Jesse to wait a minute and then slinked through the door with my magazines. Flashing what I hoped was a seductive smile, I slid them onto the desk. "I'm here to refresh the literature," I announced.

Lowell didn't even look up. "About time," he mumbled. "I still have *Playboy* with Pam Anderson's real boobs."

I gave the magazines a tiny push that sent them slipping to the floor on Lowell's side of the desk. He performed a snotty eye roll that equaled my all-time biggest and best, and then he stooped down to pick them up.

"Let me help you," I said in a voice loud enough for Jesse to hear. Out of the corner of my eye, I saw the door open, and Jesse crouched down and sneaked in as Lowell and I knelt on the floor collecting magazines.

"Wicked tie, Lowell," I commented as I tried to draw his attention to my pathetic cleavage.

"It's Gaultier," he pronounced in the French way.

I now knew cleavage was not the answer, so I switched tracks. "Madonna's favorite designer," I whispered in awe. I pictured Jesse jiggling handles, trying to find an empty donor room.

"Blessed be her name," Lowell answered as we moved to loading magazines to the desk. He was almost smiling at me when the intercom buzzed. He held up a "hold on" finger.

"What is it, Room Eight?" he snapped. "Wait a sec, I don't remember filling room eight."

"You did," I reminded him. "When I was outside, I heard you yelling to someone, 'Take room eight.'"

"Whatever," Lowell muttered.

Jesse's voice came blasting through the intercom. "The good pages are stuck together. Can I get another magazine?"

I held up a *Lusty Busty.* Lowell mouthed a silent "Yecch" as he grabbed it. "Hold that stroke, sailor," he hissed.

As soon as he darted from behind the desk and down the hall, I began flipping through the file drawers. The files were labeled with the year and the donor number, and the most recent were in the drawer I opened. I barely had time to figure that out and snap it closed when Lowell reappeared, all chatty and ready to pick up our conversation.

"I have three sealed copies of her *Sex* book," he confided.

"Oh! My! God! I'm eating my heart out," I moaned.

The intercom buzzed again.

"I need help. I can't get the video to play," complained Jesse.

"It's broken, Eight!" barked Lowell. "Flip the magazine pages fast. It'll look like a movie."

"Do you have *Big Boob Babes,* July?" asked Jesse.

"I'm gonna trade one book for concert tickets," Lowell announced to me, ignoring Jesse.

"Front row," I assured him.

Jesse buzzed again. "Please, I need it!" he pleaded over the intercom.

Lowell shot me an exasperated look, grabbed a few magazines, and flew down the hall. I made it through three file drawers before I heard him shouting, "Don't call me again, Eight, or something bad will happen!"

Lowell joined me behind the desk as I slyly pushed the magazines to the floor again.

"Are you spastic or something?" he snipped.

"So, so sorry," I apologized. I picked up a small pile as I saw Jesse bend down and slip out the front door. "I have to go," I sang out and dashed through the door.

"I'm gonna go give Eight some crap now," Lowell called after me. "Ta-ta."

It must have been a full minute before we heard him screaming for "Security!"

We raced to the van and found Gabe leaning against

it, talking to a stoner-looking dude who was eating out of a giant jar of pickle relish marked PROPERTY OF WORTHINGTON-FLAX CATERING.

"Did you know this contains all three food groups—green, red, and yellow?" he was saying as Jesse and I pulled up.

"Go! Go! Go!" I ordered Gabe as Jesse and I slid open the doors and jumped inside.

He backed up as the stoner pulled out ahead of us in his truck.

"We are so screwed," I told them. "The files only go back to 1998. They must have stored the rest somewhere else."

"So that means we're shut out, right?" said Jesse.

"Maybe not," Gabe announced.

He pointed to the writing on the back of the stoner's truck: ACME RECORD STORAGE.

"Poor guy had the munchies, and I found a jar of pickle relish in the back of the van for him. I think he might be grateful."

Ten minutes later we were waiting outside Acme Record Storage, watching Gabe exchange a cool handshake with the stoner, who still held the relish jar. Under Gabe's arm was a folder marked "Donor 908-1992." Who knew "the nerd" could be so deliciously devious?

chapter eight

Gabe parked the van so we could concentrate on reading the computer printout that was in the folder. When Jesse and I started fighting about who would get to read it out loud and grabbing the folder out of each other's hands, Gabe announced that he would do it. He opened it slowly and waited for us to give him our complete attention. "His name," he stated solemnly, "is Willard Pinchekus."

"Willard Pinchekus," I breathed. "Our biological father, Willard."

"We're the Pinchekus kids," said Jesse in wonder.

"His occupation is or was 'student.' His hobbies were origami, working out, reading, linguistics, and music," Gabe went on.

"I knew he'd be musical," I said. "That's why my mom probably picked him. She was president of the Michael Bolton Fan Club."

"I wouldn't call what that dude sings *music*," Jesse commented, probably just to piss me off.

"I'll have you know that dude started out singing lead in a cool, hard-rock band called Blackjack. He used his real name back then, Michael Bolotin. But I have to admit I kind of agree with you, Swimmy," I conceded. "Once he changed his name, he got kinda cheesy."

"Origami would have hooked my moms," Jessie continued, with a slight smirk to acknowledge the fact that he had scored a point by getting me to agree. "They're both big on napkin folding. And 'working out' probably means he was a great athlete but he was too cool to say it."

"He went to Harvard. He's got two degrees," Gabe continued. "So he was definitely super smart."

"Do they list his blood type?" I asked in a shaky voice.

"They do," Gabe answered. Then, while we held our breath, he exploded into a sneezing fit. "I think I'm allergic to the paper or the print," he panted.

"Whatever!" I shouted. "What's his blood type?"

"It's A!" Gabe yelled triumphantly.

We all screamed "Yes!" and pumped the air.

"Is his phone number listed?" I asked, pulling out my cell. "Yes, it is," said Gabe.

"Are we ready?" I asked. "Should I do it?"

"Wait," Jessie said, holding up his hand. "When you get him, put him on speaker phone."

"Of course I will," I barked.

"I'm kinda scared," Gabe whispered hoarsely. "I'm scared he'll be pissed at us for finding him."

"I'm scared he'll think I'm just a dumb jock," Jesse mumbled. "I won't let that happen, trust me," Gabe offered, giving Jess a manly pat on the shoulder. "You okay, KT?"

"As okay as someone whose dream may be shattered at any moment can be," I cracked, feeling terrified.

"Let's just do it before we chicken out," Gabe announced.

He read the numbers as I dialed and then held the phone up, on speaker, so we could all hear 908's voice. After a few rings, we heard instead the voice of a recorded operator saying, "That number has been disconnected."

"Let's try going to his address," Gabe suggested. "Maybe he still lives there, and he just changed his phone number." He read off the street and number, and Jesse and I kept repeating it like a chant so we'd be sure to get it right. Twenty minutes later we pulled up in front of it. "It" was a Starbucks. We'd struck out again.

We sat there for a minute or two, not knowing what to say. I felt my heart sinking to the pit of my stomach. Now it was really over. Then Gabe piped up with, "I bet Harvard keeps a record of all their alumni. Maybe we should try calling them."

"Not a bad thought," I said. "Let me see the printout."

He handed it over and my eyes lit up with hope. "The number for Harvard is right here," I told them. "But wait a minute. He spelled it wrong. Didn't you notice, Gabe, he spelled it 'Horvard'?"

"It's probably just his handwriting," Jesse offered. "I have lousy handwriting. Sometimes my 'a' looks like an 'o'."

I dialed the number and held up the phone again. It rang about ten times before someone picked it up. In the background I could hear cats meowing, little dogs yapping, and what sounded like a television set tuned to *The Jerry Springer Show.* Then a voice with a weird English accent said, "Horvard University. This is Dr. Cedric Pidgeon. How can I help you?"

"I would like to get the address and phone number of one of your alumni," I answered, trying to sound older. "A Willard Pinchekus."

"Of course," the dude answered. "Doctor Pinchekus is one of our most illustrious graduates. He has completed two degrees and currently is working on another one in . . ." We heard the rustling of paper, a cat meowing angrily, and the sound of little cat nails hitting the floor. "Kinesiology."

"That sounds impressive."

"Would you be interested in a degree?" the dude asked. "We offer a veritable cornucopia of courses from the 'Artistry of Auras: Viewing, Identifying, and Understanding' to 'Working with Your Animal Allies,

Teachers, and Totems.'"

"I don't think I'm interested in a course right now," I said. "I'd just like to get Doctor Pinchekus's address and phone number, please."

"I don't have his phone number, but we forward his documents and alumni quarterly to 1699 Mountain Top Road, Sedona, Arizona," he responded. "You're sure you wouldn't like a brochure, perhaps for the future?"

"No thanks, but thank you for the address," I said.

"That was not Harvard," Jesse announced.

"Duh! So he's a Horvard grad, not a Harvard grad. It's not *his* fault everybody read it wrong. He's still our bio dad, and I'm gonna get his number and call him," I continued.

"I'm with you. Go for it, KT," Gabe said encouragingly. "I don't care where he went to school. My dad almost didn't graduate from high school, and he's really, really smart."

"Yeah, whatever. The Harvard thing scared me a little," Jesse chimed in. "It gave me a lot to live up to."

I called information only to find that Willard Pinchekus's phone was unlisted. It was a bummer, but it made our next decision easy. We looked at each other and actually smiled. No one had to say a word. We still had major issues with each other, but we all knew exactly where we were going.

chapter nine

When I got home, Kim was cuddling in front of the TV with Ben, her latest squeeze. She jumped up to greet me, checked out my candy striper threads, and shot me a puzzled look.

"It's for the band," I explained. "We're called 'Krash Kart' now. It's spelled with two Ks."

"You look nice, Katie," Kim said. "Very wholesome. Where did you . . . were you in my closet?"

Ben cleared his throat.

"You remember . . ."

"Ben. Yeah, hi."

"It's Ken," he mumbled. "I brought my blender over."

"That was very thoughtful, Ken. Thanks. By the way, Mom, I'm going to Sasha's tomorrow and staying over for the whole week so we can rehearse. I've got my cell and my charger."

"Okay, honey. Check in with me, though, will you? Sometimes when I call you there, you can't hear the phone over the music. Give my regards to Sasha's mom and dad and don't forget to thank them when you leave."

"I won't forget," I said.

She and Ken smiled at me and watched me walk away, but they were locking lips before I even opened the door to my room. How annoying was that?

I called Sasha right away and filled her in on my sad sib situation, the Willard discovery, and the expedition to Sedona in search of our dad.

"Where are the moms and the Butcherellis?" she wanted to know.

"The moms are gone for two weeks catering a wedding in the Bahamas. Then when they come back, they're gonna divide the spatulas and split up."

"Somebody got a new somebody?"

"Not according to Jesse. They've lost the heat. Maybe they need mama drama. Whatever it is, it isn't a good thing."

"And the Butchies?"

"They won a cruise in a ballroom dancing contest. They'll be sambaing up a storm for ten days, so if you'll say I'm with you, we're all in the clear."

"I'll cover for you, K," Sasha assured me. "But how are you getting to Arizona?"

"Jesse has his moms' wheels while they're away, so we're driving. That's the only reason I'm hanging with them. Seems I'm stuck with them if I want to hook up with Willard."

"KT Pinchekus, it does have a ring to it," Sasha mused.

"We're leaving in the morning, so you have to answer your phone every time it rings. If it's my mom, tell her I'm out getting a pizza or a guitar string or something, and text or call me immediately, if not sooner."

"I can figure out the drill," Sasha told me. "Hey, I'm really excited for you. Willard's gonna be very cool, and it's all gonna be good."

I wanted to believe her. But I just said, "Did you have a salad at McDonald's?"

"Of course, I did," she answered, too enthusiastically. "And my dad liked the Kings. Caleb was amazing."

I didn't believe her for a minute about the salad, but she was covering for me. I figured I'd work on her eating habits when I got back.

"Thanks, Sash," I said.

"Good luck, K," she answered. "Check in, will ya?"

I agreed to, and with that out of the way, I lay down on my bed and daydreamed about Willard and what he would be like. I said a little prayer (even though I'm not religious) that he'd be glad we found him and not slam the door in our faces. And then I realized that I was really lucky to have brothers instead of sisters because I'd be his only "little girl" and probably his favorite. Then I picked up my guitar and wrote a song called "My Little Girl." It was kind of country rock, about how this dad was always going to be there for his daughter even after he gave her away at her wedding. It was mushier than most of my stuff, but it came from my heart. I felt like, all in all, this had been a really good day until about ten o'clock. I was in my pjs, packing my backpack, when I heard a guitar and a voice outside my window. It was Dylan, singing:

"I'm addicted to you,
You make my head spin.
You're the reason
For the crazy state my heart is in.
Nobody loves you like me, KT.
Nobody loves you like me."

I opened my window and there he was, leaning against a tree, looking as if being there at ten o'clock at night was the most natural thing in the world. When he saw me, his face lit up. If he'd had a tail, he would have wagged it.

"You gotta get over me already, Dylan, like now," I told him. "There must be some kind of love rehab place you can go to."

"But I like the way I feel about you," he said. "It feels warm and good. I don't want to get over it."

"You have to, and you're gonna have to go cold turkey," I answered. "My brothers and I are going to Sedona."

"You're going to Sedona with Butcherelli and Jesse the jock? Why?"

"Number 806 wasn't our dad. Our dad lives in Sedona, and we're going to find him. So goodbye, Dylan. Please go home now."

I slammed the window shut and pulled down the shade. Then I threw my phone and charger into my backpack and zipped it closed, but something told me that I wasn't in the clear. I listened quietly for a few seconds. "You're still out there, aren't you?" I asked.

"Yes, I am," I heard through the window. "I'm just going to sit here for a while being happy for you. You can go to sleep."

I let out a silent scream, turned out the light, jumped into bed, and pulled the covers over my head. I hoped I would fall asleep right away because I couldn't wait for tomorrow.

chapter ten

When Gabe and I got to Jesse's at nine in the morning, he was totally torqued off and manic. I didn't know that laid-back Swimmy had that much fire in him. It seems his moms had taken off for the Bahamas on a 7:00 a.m. flight while he was sleeping. They'd left him a note saying that they were parking the car at the airport and had taken the van in for servicing while they were away. They'd left him home-cooked frozen dinners for every night they'd be gone, in addition to extra money for taxis and buses, and said that he should stay close to home. We were all packed, and now we were without wheels. I guess Jesse knew he was on the hook because he looked like he was about to go postal.

"Let's rent a car," I suggested. Somehow the nuttier he got, the calmer I got, even though I wanted to kill him and his moms.

"You have to be at least twenty-one to rent a car," he snapped. "I thought you knew everything."

"Whoa, Big Feller," I said, "If we can't rent one, then how 'bout we steal one?"

"Like you'd know how," Jesse said scornfully.

"We could borrow one," the Wimpy One volunteered.

"From who?" Jesse asked.

"From my dad," said Gabe. "He's got a car repair shop. He and my mom are on their cruise, and they gave me the key to the lot so I can check on things."

"Good thinking, Batman," I said. "I didn't think you harbored even a speck of larceny in your skinny little soul."

"You're at the bottom of the learning curve when it comes to me," Gabe said. That line was pretty impressive for him.

"Ding dong!" I said. "The witch is dead . . . for now. So tell me, Houdini, how do we pull off this caper?"

"Just follow me," he directed, picking up his ratty overnight bag.

I slung my backpack over my shoulder and picked up my guitar case as Jesse pulled out a suitcase with initials all over it. I've always wondered why people wanted stuff with other people's initials on it. He saw the way I was looking at it.

"My moms got it for me. I didn't ask them for it. I didn't want it. It's all I've got."

"My sympathies," I said, and we headed for the door.

⁑ ⁑ ⁑

We took the bus, and on the way, we pooled our money. Jesse's moms had left him two hundred dollars. I had $70 of birthday and babysitting money, and Gabe had $87.50. I had already stocked up on NoDoz, so we had plenty of cash for gas and food until we got to Sedona. Then I read them the driving schedule I had worked out.

Jesse, of course, told me that we didn't need a schedule, which made no sense at all since we couldn't agree on almost anything. So I told him since no one else had bothered to organize the trip, this schedule trumped no schedule, so my schedule was it.

We got off the bus and walked three blocks to Butcherelli Muffler and Auto Repair. It was a neat little operation with two hoists, a bunch of cars parked outside in a gated area, and a small office that looked like a little house.

Gabe let us in with the key, and we checked out everything on the lot. There were oversized SUVs (I wouldn't be caught dead in one), vans, sedans, and sports cars. We finally picked a cherry-red Prius that looked almost new. Then we went into the office to get the key.

There was a case with a glass front. All the car keys were hanging inside it on little hooks with numbers. Gabe tried to open it with the key we used to get into the lot, but it wouldn't turn. We jiggled and tried forcing it, but it wasn't the right key. There was no way we could make it be the right key, and I was beginning to panic.

"Don't freak yet, KT," Gabe said. "I've got an idea."

"I hope it's better than this one," I said.

"Just go out and count the cars in the lot," he directed me. "Why me?" I asked. "Don't you think Jesse can count?"

"It was random, KT. You can stay here, and Jesse can count the cars."

"I'll go," I said.

It took all of twenty seconds to walk out, count, and come back.

"Thirteen cars," I told him.

"Bingo!" said Jesse. "There are twelve keys in the case. That means one of the cars has the keys in it."

"I sure underestimated you, Mr. Hawking," I quipped.

"Not funny, KT," Gabe whispered through clenched teeth.

We ran out and started jiggling door handles. Nothing opened, and then we spotted it. Over in the corner, looking as if it had been put there to die, was a Jeep Wrangler, ten years old at least, the kind with the plastic windows. It must have been green once, but it was so dilapidated and scratched that you couldn't really call it any color. The soft top was shredded, and the door creaked open the minute I tried it. The key was on the floor, not even under the mat. Who would have wanted to steal this wreck?

"We're not gonna discuss it. Let's see if it has gas," Gabe suggested and turned the key in the ignition. It was half full, which was the only good news about it. He snorted some nasal spray, sneezed, coughed, and pasted a Breathe-Rite on his nose. Now all was well in his world.

"Let's go," said Jesse.

He tried putting his suitcase behind the back seat, but it didn't fit. We ended up putting Gabe's little bag there and stacking everything else, including my guitar, in the back seat next to me. Jesse got into the shotgun seat, and Gabe got behind the wheel. He whipped out a huge box of tissues for Jesse to hold so he could be fed a constant supply.

"We're off to see the Willard," Jesse began singing. It was something that I might have done. I actually smiled, but I was glad that nobody saw it.

chapter eleven

We gassed up, picked up lots of snacks, and headed for the interstate. I pulled out my pad to go over the driving schedule again. "So, to recap, Gabe drives and Jesse navigates until we get to empty. Then we fill up, I drive, and Gabe copilots. Then . . ."

Jesse cut in. "Jesse drives until blah, blah, blah. You've gone over it three times, KT. Could you be a touch controlling?"

"Some people don't look like they're really listening," I countered. Truth was, I didn't think he'd ever remember it, and I admit to being something of a control freak.

By this time we were caught in traffic and creeping up the ramp to the interstate. Jesse was turning in his seat to face me so we could get into it for real, when something caught his eye.

"Hey," he said, "check out that guy. Maybe we could pick him up. He could help drive and pay for gas."

"He looks cool," Gabe agreed.

I looked out of the window, and there, holding up a sign that read SEDONA, ARIZONA, OR CLOSE was Dylan. He looked so cute and hopeful that I wanted to shoot him on the spot. I held up my pad to hide my face and scrunched down in the seat.

"There's no room back here," I snapped. "Besides, that's a serial killer if I ever saw one."

The traffic opened up and we zoomed past him. I couldn't believe that after everything I'd said to him, Dylan was following me to Arizona. I told myself that it was creepy, but somewhere, way deep inside, I felt guilty for thinking that, because it was really kind of sweet. I knew he wanted to look out for me (not that I needed it).

We'd been on the highway for a few hours, and Gabe was going under the speed limit when a cop car in the next lane stayed even with us. We could see that they were checking us out.

"We better get off at the next exit," Gabe said. "I only have an intermediate license."

"Me, too," Jesse said. "So what?"

"Read the fine print," Gabe answered. "'You may not operate a motor vehicle with more than three passengers who are under nineteen years old and who are not members of your immediate family.'"

"We are family. Unfortunately," I said.

"The cops will never believe that one," Jesse scoffed. "We all have different last names on our IDs."

"Yeah, get off as soon as you can," I told Gabe. "We don't even have registration for this heap."

"She's right for once," Jesse chimed in. "We gotta take the back roads."

"I know how to get to Route 66," Gabe said, heading for the off-ramp. "My folks and I took it to visit my uncle in Tulsa last year."

"Did you have the best time ever?" I asked in a slightly snarky tone.

"Yeah," Gabe replied. "My uncle taught me some new magic tricks, and I have two cousins I really like."

"I don't get it," I said. "Why are you even going on this trip? I need a dad. Jesse needs a home. Why do you even care about Willard?"

"I told you, KT. Sometimes you're the one who doesn't really listen. I'm looking for the same reason you are. I want to know all of me. My dad is okay with it, too. He said that when they got back from their cruise, we'd talk about finding my biological father. But I didn't want to wait. I thought I'd rather go with you 'cause with all I've got at home, I don't have any brothers or sisters. It's just easier doing it with you guys because we're all looking for the same thing, really. We all want to feel like we're more than the result of some petri dish experiment, like we really belong in the world, just like everyone else. That's why I care, KT."

"I get it," I mumbled and then changed the subject by pointing to a sign. "Hey, look, if we weren't in such a hurry, we could visit the culture capitol of Missouri, The Riverside Reptile Ranch."

"I've been there," said Jesse. "Some of my friends think it's a cool first-date place 'cause girls get all clingy around reptiles."

"I'm gonna remember that in case I ever have a date," Gabe piped in.

"It's so messed up that we're related. What kind of male chauvinist crap are you teaching him, Swimmy? You're dealing with an impressionable mind," I grumbled.

"I didn't say that I thought so," Jesse snapped. "I just said some of my friends did."

"If you're different, then why are you friends with them?" I wanted to know.

"Sometimes people are friends with other people because it just works out that way. Everybody needs people to hang out with in school."

"Yeah," said Gabe, "I hang out with the nerds because they're the only ones who want me."

"Do nerds know that people think they're nerds?" I asked.

"Everyone knows who people think they are, but sometimes that's not all they are," Gabe answered.

"No shit," Jesse said.

He and Gabe locked eyes for a "got ya" minute, and I got it, too, but I decided to refrain from comment on this whole male bonding moment.

We stopped at the next gas station, filled up the tank, and peed. When I came back to the car, Gabe was demonstrating his "Up in Smoke" trick to a bunch of wide-eyed kids. He seemed to be controlling the smoke element better because no one was choking or coughing. When Jesse finally appeared and took in what was going on, we looked at each other and rolled our eyes. The trick was so feeble it was embarrassing.

"Could you make yourself go up in smoke, bro?" Jesse asked him. "That's a Copperfield trick I've never tried," Gabe answered. "Give it a shot sometime," suggested Jesse.

"Show's over, folks," I announced, and the kids scattered as we piled into the Jeep.

I got behind the wheel and motioned for Gabe to sit next to me. Jesse scrunched into the back seat and curled up with his varsity jacket over his head.

"Wake me up when it's my turn to drive," he said.

I gunned the engine, leaned on the accelerator, and we zoomed out of the gas station. Within minutes Jesse was snoring. Then he began to fart and kept it up until we had to stop and zip out the windows. If I had smell-o-vision on my phone, I would have made a video.

chapter twelve

We barreled through Oklahoma. I had my foot as close to the floor as I could get it, while Gabe kept an eye out for patrol cars. Then he asked me in a kind of shy voice, "Can I ask you some questions?"

"About what?" I asked.

"About girls. Like what do they like to talk about?"

"I don't have a clue," I told him, and then I paused and thought it wouldn't hurt to be more sisterly. "I'm not exactly your guru on girls."

"I don't expect you to be a guru, but you are a girl," Gabe said patiently. "So what do you like? Glasses or contacts, for example. I'm looking for an overview. Just tell me what you like."

"I honestly don't know. At this moment I would say nothing. The way I see it is, relationships suck. They're like roadside bombs. Sooner or later they blow up and somebody always gets hurt."

"Has anyone told you that you can sound kind of bitter?" Gabe asked gently.

"Oh Gabe, my innocent brother. Some people might say that, but I would say I actually sound like a realist."

He didn't ask any more questions after that and I was glad. Whenever I went over sixty, the Jeep made weird, scary noises so I wanted to concentrate on driving. I didn't care what it did, though, as long as it didn't break down. I just wanted to get to my dad as soon as possible, and that thought was like a magnet pulling me toward Sedona.

I had to slow down through OK City, but we made great time. About midnight I pulled over at a rest stop just west of the city. We decided not to tell Jesse about the farting (which everyone does at one time or another) unless he asked why the windows were gone, which he didn't.

Gabe and I bought some vending machine sandwiches, and Jesse remembered he had a BLT in his bag and whipped it out.

"Mmm, Jesse. Dead pig slabs with wilted lettuce and warm mayo. How yum!"

"Thanks for that, sis," he answered as he began chomping in the most revolting way possible.

I couldn't wait to crawl into the back seat and conk out.

So when he finished his disgusting sandwich and took the wheel, that's what I did. When I woke up and looked at my watch, it was 5:30 a.m., and I wondered why we weren't moving. I checked the front seats. Gabe and Jesse were both gone so I got out to look for them. There they were, standing in the middle of what looked like a cow pasture, looking really small against the big gray and orange sky.

Gabe was rubbing the sleep from his eyes, and the sun was rising over ten graffiti-covered Cadillacs, half-buried, nose-down in the ground. It looked like something out of a bizarre dream.

"Where are we?" Gabe was saying as I tiptoed silently behind them to hear their conversation.

"I dunno exactly," Jesse answered. "Somewhere near Amarillo, Texas."

"You were driving, dude. I must have passed out," Gabe yawned.

"You were my navigator. What good is a sleeping navigator? I've got no sense of direction, bro. I already told you that. I saw this sign for Cadillac Ranch and thought it must be a Texas car dealer in civilization with gas and food. Instead it's these cars stuck in the ground in the middle of nowhere," Jesse said, sounding panicked. "She'll freak when she wakes up, not being on the schedule and all. Damn, she's the only girl I've ever been scared of."

"She's the only girl I've ever not been scared of. This is very cool, and she's weird. Maybe she'll get it," Gabe offered.

"This place is too creepy even for her. Is this a Cadillac graveyard? It could be haunted by all the people who died in

Cadillacs, and I promise you, she's not gonna get anything when she finds out we're kind of out of gas."

"Out of *gas,*" I echoed. They both jumped.

Jesse gulped. "Hi," he said.

"Morning, KT," Gabe chirped, trying to sound cheerful.

"This isn't a gas station," Jesse observed guiltily.

I looked around. "You're right for once, Jess," I said pleasantly. "Excuse me, please."

I disappeared behind one of the Cadillacs and started banging on it with my fists screaming, "Shit! Shit! Shit!" for a few minutes. When I had gotten it all out of my system, I walked out from behind the Caddy calmly, wearing a manic smile. "I think we should go back to the road and wait . . . perhaps for days . . . for a car to come along," I said quietly.

"That's a plan. Good idea. Let's do that," they babbled nervously.

We walked back to the road and nobody said a word. When the sun came up, it felt like we were human Hot Pockets being nuked inside a microwave. There wasn't a cloud in the sky and heat waves shimmered in the air.

I got my guitar out of the backseat and sat down at the side of the dusty road. I started singing "Cadillac Ranch," which is a really good song by Bruce Springsteen, another old-guy rock guitar player and singer. I couldn't stop playing it, even though I knew I was driving the guys nuts. I didn't really care, though, because I felt they deserved it.

Gabe took out his box of magic stuff and practiced new lame tricks while Jesse lay down by the side of the road with his T-shirt over his face. It was like he thought if he couldn't see us, we couldn't see him.

After a couple of hours, we were all doing absolutely nothing, just sitting there, blankly staring down the road, waiting for someone to show up. Then, suddenly, Gabe jumped up.

"Look!" he yelled, pointing down the road.

"It's a mirage," I croaked.

Coming toward us, out of the sun, was a car. A beautiful, beautiful car. We all started cheering until it got close enough to see what it was. It was just what we had been trying to avoid: the cops. The Texas Highway Patrol, to be exact.

We looked at each other in total panic, but there was no time to say anything before the car pulled up in a cloud of dust and a ginormous trooper got out.

"Hey," he said. "You kids okay?"

"Absolutely, Officer, sir," Jesse answered. "We just have a slight gas problem."

"Yeah," Gabe added. "We're out of it."

"No problem. No way," grinned the big man. "I got me an extra few gallons on board for emergencies like this. You just pull out your driver's license and registration, sonny, and we'll have you on your way."

"Uh, it's in the car," Jesse stalled. And we all rushed over to the Jeep.

"I'll go get it with him, he can never find anything!" I yelled over my shoulder to the lawman. "What are we gonna do? What are we gonna do?" I babbled to the boys, losing my cool completely. "When he sees Jesse's license, he'll take us straight to the slammer and call our parents. We're totally screwed."

"Cool it, KT. I got an idea," Gabe whispered as we pretended to rummage around in the Jeep. "When he brings out the gas, Jess, you keep him busy for a minute and then leave it to me. KT, you get in the car, behind the wheel, and wait."

"For what?" I wanted to know.

"You'll see," Gabe said calmly. "Just be ready to jam it!"

"Get a move on, kids. I want to make it home for breakfast," the trooper called over to us, setting down a plastic container of gas next to our fill spout.

"I can't find my license. Could ya help me look for it? I must have dropped it when I was laying in the grass," Jesse called back, heading for the side of the road.

The cop followed him. "I'm a tellin' you, sonny, you better find it, 'cause if you ain't got proper license and registration, I gotta take you in, and I gotta take your car in. And what's worse is, I gotta miss breakfast and my wife's makin' apple fritters."

As Jesse and the cop searched in the grass, Gabe quickly filled the tank with the gas in the container. I sat behind the wheel, wondering what was going to happen next.

"I found it, Jesse!" yelled Gabe. "It was behind the seat."

Jesse looked bewildered, and the cop looked relieved as they headed back to where Gabe was standing now, between the Jeep and the patrol car. I could tell that Jesse was scared out of his head, and the cop was smelling the fritters and grinning.

"I got his license," Gabe said. "My sister's looking for the registration. Wanna see a magic trick while we wait?"

They moved closer to the cop car, and Gabe kept looking at Jesse as if they could telecommunicate.

"Thanks, but no thanks. Hand over the license, boy, I gotta run it."

"You'll love the trick, I promise," Gabe said, moving closer to the cop.

"Yur gettin' me aggervated, son," the cop drawled. "You're missin' a good chance to shut up."

"Okay," Gabe agreed.

And that was the last thing anyone said before he rubbed his hands together and more smoke than he'd ever made before billowed out of them. It enveloped the cop in a dark gray cloud, and he was coughing and waving his arms as Jesse grabbed the car keys from the police cruiser and flung them into the grass. Then he and Gabe jumped into our car and I gunned the engine. The Jeep screeched and shuddered so much I thought it would fall apart. But we went screaming down the road and were out of there before the smoke even cleared.

We turned down a side road after a few miles just in case the law was following us, and I pulled over onto the shoulder. Then Jesse and I started pumping our fists and slapping Gabe on the back, totally jazzed. I'd never seen the nerd look that happy. We kept reliving the whole crazy adventure as we hightailed it through the Texas sticks.

For the next half hour, I almost forgot that it was Jesse's brainlessness that got us into the whole mess in the first place. Then the Jeep started coughing and we rolled to a stop. The lawman had given us just enough gas to get to a station on the highway, but now we were nowhere near the highway. We were fugitives from the law, hiding out on a deserted back road, miles from nowhere, with the sun blazing, the tumbleweed tumbling, the temperatures soaring, and not a gas station in sight. My memory was suddenly restored. I remembered very clearly whose fault it was that we were here, and you can be sure I brought it to Jesse's attention until he wished he were roadkill.

chapter thirteen

I kept reminding Swimmy that he was the one who had gotten us into this as we pushed the Jeep down the desolate winding road through the hot, dry swelter. I was guiding the wheel and pushing, so I probably was carrying the least weight, but my shoulder began to feel like it was about to fall off. There was only the dust, the sun, the damn tumbleweed, and us. I swear, it must have been a hundred and ten degrees, and it wasn't even ten in the morning.

It was possibly the most uncomfortable and annoying situation I have ever been in. Sweat kept rolling down my forehead into my eyes, my feet were blistering, and I could feel the cancer rays burning through my shorts and T-shirt.

Maybe I was going nuts from the heat, but I kept wondering if it would be justifiable homicide if I murdered Jesse.

Then I came to my senses and realized we needed him to help push since he was the strongest. I didn't even have the strength to yell at him anymore; my throat was too dry. Instead, I whispered, "I've always wondered what hell would be like and now I know, thanks to the two of you."

"Somebody said you go to heaven for the climate and hell for the company," chirped Gabe.

"Whoever said that was wrong," I mumbled.

"Listen, KT, I said I was sorry. I made a mistake." Jesse grunted as he pushed. "It was a big one, but beating me up every minute isn't going to change anything."

He was right. The dopey jock had finally said something intelligent. I had no retort, so I just shut up.

Finally, after half an hour that felt like half a day, past a sign that pointed to Vega and Adrian, we saw something up ahead slowly becoming visible through the glare. We all croaked a hoarse cheer. It was a gas station, right there, in what seemed like the middle of nowhere. A beautiful, run-down gas station that wasn't too run-down to have gas. As an added attraction, it had a convenience store that was sure to have something cold to drink.

The sight of salvation made us push harder. Then the road started to slope downward slightly, and the pushing became easier. The good news turned to bad when the Jeep began picking up speed, and then we realized it was taking us along with it instead of the other way around. Soon we were hanging on to the Jeep as it rolled. We peeled off one by one as it picked up speed and watched helplessly as it headed for the gas pumps.

"The whole place is gonna blow!" Jesse shouted as he dropped to the ground. We followed suit, closed our eyes, slapped our hands over our ears, and waited for the explosion. But all we heard was the "I'm here" bell as the Jeep glided into the station and came to rest as close to the pump as if someone had parked it there. Gabe had turned very white as the car coasted toward oblivion, but his color came back when he saw it was safe. The three of us got up and raced down to the station, high-fiving all the way.

As we checked out our car, the door to the convenience store opened, and a string bean of a dude moseyed out. He was weathered and grizzled and had a face that looked like a truck had backed into it—kind of like Keith Richards, the old-guy guitar player in The Stones who played the great riff on "I Can't Get No Satisfaction," a song I personally embrace as an anthem. Anyway, he looked like Keith if Keith had stringy gray hair and a straggly beard and was munching a gas station sandwich.

"Howdy," he said, smiling. He held out his hand for a shake, and we each shook it because it seemed like he really wanted that to happen. He kept on grinning. His tooth situation was hit or miss, and what few he still owned had tobacco stains all over them.

"Y'all look parched," he observed, tossing a can of cold Dr. Pepper at us. I caught it on the fly, guzzled some, and passed it on.

"Thanks," Jesse gulped. "You the owner?"

"Think I'd be hangin' out in this godforsaken place if I weren't?" the guy asked with a grin. "Whut's ailin' yer jalopy, there?"

"We're just out of gas," Gabe told him.

He looked us over. "Y'all look plum wore out. Go ahead on inside and cool off whilst I fill 'er up fer ya. I got some tasty sandwiches in thar, and Coke in the cooler right next to some ice cold *cerveza*. Hep yurselves on me."

"*Cerveza* is beer," Gabe translated. "He's giving us beer, you guys."

"That's a little too nice of you," I said. "What's the real deal?"

"Hell, this is Texas, kids. Ain't you ever heard of Texas hospitality?" he chuckled. "Looks like you got yourselves in one fine pickle, and you need some help."

"You're on the money," I admitted.

"Besides, I have every intention of overchargin' you fer the gas."

That made us all laugh. We were so hot, exhausted, and thirsty, our brains were fried. Jesse kept mumbling, "I want a beer" like he was some kind of underage alky, so we trudged into the convenience store with our last bit of energy. It was nice and cool and kind of dark, and there was even music with a pounding bass drum playing from a boom box on the counter. We each grabbed a drink and a sandwich. Mine was plain cheese, and I scraped off the mayo. Then we collapsed onto a bench and leaned against the wall. Gabe and I had Cokes and Jesse grabbed a Corona.

I had taken my phone out of my backpack, but I couldn't even get one bar. I figured I'd call home later and leave a message on my mom's voicemail, telling her Sasha and I were working on a new song together. Then we munched and drank and listened to the radio.

"I gotta say it again. I'm sorry," Jesse said from out of nowhere. "If I hadn't made that dumb mistake, we wouldn't be here."

"It's not so bad," Gabe answered. "We're okay now and this sandwich is excellent."

"Everybody makes mistakes," I admitted finally. "I'm possibly a little impatient sometimes."

"We can't all be as cool or as smart as you, KT," Jesse offered.

"You think I'm cool?" I was amazed. "You're the cool one, Swimmy. Mr. Perfect Swim Star with his own groupies."

"That's not cool. Cool is knowing who you are and being that, no matter what anyone else thinks," Jesse sighed.

"People at school say you could be the next Michael Phelps. You could win a bunch of Olympic medals," Gabe piped in. "And if that isn't cool, I don't know what is."

"Thanks for thinking that, but no, I couldn't be another Phelps. I'm good for high school, but I'm not great, and I don't love it all that much. It's just all I know how to do at this point." He held the chilled Corona against his forehead. "Actually, I don't know who I am or what I'm good at or what

I want to do or even what I'm doing here on this planet."

For a dumb jock, Swimmy was getting more profound by the minute. Shockingly, I knew exactly what he meant. Sometimes I had the feeling that I didn't know why I was here, but then I'd pick up my guitar and that feeling would go away. I was starting to feel bad for him, and it was weird. He was almost kind of relatable.

I walked over to the boom box, which was pounding out some bass-heavy disco song, and lowered the volume. Funny thing was, when the song got lower, the bass stayed at the same level.

"That thumping isn't a bass drum," I announced. "Something freaky is going on."

We followed the sound, and it kept getting louder as we headed to the back of the store. We walked out the rear door and followed the thumping to the bathroom. It was definitely coming from there. We jiggled the handle but it was locked. Then Gabe looked down and saw the key on the ground.

"That's funny," he mumbled, unlocking the door and pushing it open.

Inside was a dude with his arms and legs tied and his mouth duct taped. He was laying on the floor, kicking the wall to get attention, and those kicks were making the bass-drum sound. We were all over him in a second, untying him and pulling the tape off his mouth. The first thing he did was grab the beer Jesse was holding and chug it.

"He still here?" he wanted to know.

"Who?" we all asked.

"Howdy, shake, tie up, and rob. That's who," the dude answered. "The skinny, old, white guy. He cleaned out the register and cut the phone line."

"So he's not the owner?" Jesse asked.

"I'm Carlos, and I own this place. You got a cell?"

"I can't get a signal," I told him.

"You can try mine," Jesse said. He reached into his jeans pocket. "I must have left mine in the—" And then it hit us all at the same time.

We dashed out to the pump, followed by Carlos. There was nothing and no one there. The Jeep was gone, along with the shit-kicker cowboy and all our stuff.

"You left the keys in it, KT, and he jacked our ride. I think you may have outscored me in the Stupidity Olympics," Jesse observed.

"And you may have just scored the gold in the category of Stating the Obvious."

He was so annoying, but he was right. I shouldn't have left the keys in it. I should have followed my instinct that he was being too nice. We were so screwed, and it was all my fault. I had to find some way to fix it.

"I gotta lie down," Gabe said, looking like he was gonna pass out. "If that car's gone, I'm dead. I'm a dead, dead man. My dad'll . . ." It was too much for him. He sat down with his head between his knees. It scared me. I'd never seen him without his rose-colored glasses on.

"Hey, Butchie, don't freak out on us now. We'll figure it out, and besides, we don't have time for you to fall apart."

"If we all keep it together," Jessie muttered. "We're gonna be fine.

"Listen, chicos," Carlos announced. "There's a cafe 'bout five miles down the road, and they got a phone. Call the cops from there, tell them what happened, and what your car looks like."

"And how do we get there?" I wanted to know.

"I got my pickup behind the storage shed out back. You can take that and leave it there for me," Carlos told us.

"How do you know we're not gonna steal it?" asked Jesse. "After all, we need wheels. We just got robbed."

"I got kids your age. You're normal pain-in-the-ass dumb teenagers, but you're not robbers."

"Why don't *you* go call the cops?" Gabe asked suspiciously. He was starting to come around.

"My wife is gonna be here in fifteen minutes. If Cecilia sees that I'm gone, there's no money in the register, and you're here, she'll go ballistic and call the cops. If I'm here and the cash register is empty, I have a shot at explaining before she blows her stack and something gets broken. I'm trusting you to wait for the cop car and let them take you into Adrian. They'll send someone out here and then they'll find your wheels. Ain't many places to hide near here. Now get goin'. I gotta see if he took anything else."

He tossed us his car keys. Jesse caught them and took out a ten. "This is for the Corona, some sandwiches, and three cokes."

"Keep it. Just get crackin'. And if by any chance you should decide to heist my truck, I swear I will send Cecilia after you." Carlos shuddered just thinking about that and headed for the store as we raced toward the storage shed.

Jeez, I thought. *What crappy thing is gonna happen next?*

Then as if he could read my mind, Jesse came out with, "Hang in there, KT. It's gonna be worth it when we find our bio dad."

chapter fourteen

Gabe took the wheel of Carlos' truck, Jesse and I scrunched in next to him, and we hit the road hard. After about ten minutes, I looked in the rearview mirror and saw the shape of a police car through the dust cloud tailing us.

"Damn, what are we? Cop magnets?" I muttered.

Gabe just pushed his foot down on the accelerator. "They'll never believe us when we tell them Carlos gave us this heap. They'll take us in until they can check out our story with him, and we won't get to Sedona for another day, because we'll be sitting in the hoosegow."

"I can't get busted," Jesse groaned. "I don't wanna be somebody's bitch."

"Chill, blondie," I told him. "I've got an idea. Keep your fingers crossed that I can get some reception here."

I turned on my phone, and even though I only had one bar, it was one more than I had back at the gas station. I prayed and punched 911.

"Nueve once, 911. What is your emergency?" a woman drawled.

"Hey, I'd like to report a robbery at the gas station west of Vega. Yeah, Carlos asked me to call you. His phone line is down. We're in his truck trying to head off Cecilia. You know how she is."

"We do, and we're headed for Carlos's place. Right now. *Adios.*" Behind us, the cop car spun around, sirens blaring.

"Beautiful, KT," Jesse said, breathing a sigh of relief. "You saved my ass."

"I figured the whole Adrian police force must be in that car," I grinned.

I felt like I was beginning to restore my cred and possibly make up for my screwup.

Gabe turned down another road heading west. "I think we better stay out of sight for a while, and *whoa* . . . looky here." He screeched to a stop in front of a sign that read BIKINI HANDY HAND AUTO WASH AND WAX $12 JUST 1 MILE.

"I think we oughta stop there," Jesse announced. "I have a feeling about it."

"Yeah, I know that feeling," Gabe agreed. "You wanna look at bikini babes and get a boner."

"That, too," Jesse agreed. "But honestly, it's more than that. And I mean that in a good way, so take that grossed-out look off your face, KT."

"I just want our stuff back," I said.

"I gotta get that Jeep back. It's essential to my survival," Gabe mumbled through clenched teeth and his usual stuffed-up nose. "But first I gotta get some Breathe-Rites. I'm on my last one."

"Yeah, let's stop for a second. I could use a Dr. Pepper," I added. "The Doc stimulates the problem-solving part of my brain."

The Handy Hand car wash lay ahead of us on the right. It was a sad, shabby setup. Cars and pickups rolled through the wash tunnel to be polished by girls in bikinis. Part of the property was an ancient motel with newly cleaned sets of wheels parked in front of the rooms.

We parked the truck to the side of the wash line, piled out, and waited while Gabe dashed into the tiny convenience store. He soon returned, waving a Breathe-Rite box. Meanwhile, Jesse was working his smile magic on a cute bikini babe vacuuming a car. She smiled back. "Handy hand special? Fifty bucks for you."

"The sign said twelve," Gabe reminded her. He was so totally clueless about anything to do with the opposite sex.

"Easy, Butchie Boy," I told him, "she's talking about more than buffing the fender." I was pulling them both toward the drink vending machines when Jesse stopped.

"Wait a minute," he said and turned around.

Something made us turn around, too, and there it was.

Emerging from the wash tunnel, sparkling in the sun . . . the Jeep. If life had a soundtrack, the music would have swelled.

I rubbed my eyes. "Tell me that I'm not hallucinating," I begged them.

"You're not. It's real!" they yelled, and we rushed over as another bikini babe drove it to the pickup area to be dried. We surrounded her and looked into the car. Our stuff, including my guitar, was still there, wedged into the back seat. I pulled Jesse's phone out of his charger while Jesse was doing what he did best. He flashed the babe his super smile. His face was so tan from the Texas sun, his teeth were blinding—in a good way.

"This your daddy's car?" the babe asked.

"Yup," Jesse answered. "I'm here to bring it to him." He was leaning close to her and flexing everything he had that could flex. I could have sworn that I saw his hair contracting and expanding. Gabe was watching in awe.

She kept drying the same spot on the Jeep, staring into Jesse's baby blues. "Your daddy is in room ten. He's partying with my sister. You got a yellow ticket, handsome?"

"No," he whispered in a sexy voice, "but I've got a green one." And with that, he waved a twenty in the air. She laughed and took it.

"You bad, bad boy," she giggled, tossing him the keys.

"I wish I could show you how bad," Jesse sighed as we got into the Jeep. He held out another twenty. "Hey, beautiful, get that truck we parked over there washed and dried for me, will ya? A dude named Carlos is gonna come and pick it up. Don't give it to anyone but him."

The babe stuck both twenties into her cleavage, threw Jesse a kiss, and made an A-okay sign.

"Get moving, Studley Dudley," I hissed while dialing his phone. As we pulled away, I could see the babe still waving goodbye to Swimmy in the rearview mirror.

"Hey, Senora 911," I said into Jesse's cell, "when Carlos's phone line at the gas station is working again, would you please tell him that his pickup is waiting for him at the Bikini Car Wash instead of the café, 'cause his friends were in a rush, and the wash and dry is on us? Could you do me a solid and tell him directly? I may have mentioned that if we could leave Cecilia out of the loop, it would be very cool. Yup, she can be a little *loca*. Oh by the way, FYI, the perp who robbed Carlos is at The Handy Hand in room ten as we speak. *Adios, amiga. Muchas gracias.*"

I gave the boys a thumbs-up, and Jesse hit the gas. "Yee-haw!" he whooped.

"Hot Dawg!" I yelled.

"Pinchekus kids rule!" shouted Gabe, and we all started singing "We're off to see the Willard" at the top of our lungs.

chapter fifteen

We got back on Route 66 and barreled through Glenrio, where signs of life consisted mostly of junked cars. Then we crossed into New Mexico, and I personally was really stoked to get out of Texas alive and without having committed fratricide.

The road got pretty crappy and gravelly, but it didn't slow us down. There was a hot desert breeze that only made us sweatier and more tired, and we hardly talked at all for a while. The road was littered with ghost towns and closed gas stations, so we gassed up in a place called Tucumcari and got snacks for the road. I took the wheel and Gabe navigated, while Jess munched on a bacon burger in the back seat.

"If you get anything meat-related on my guitar case, Swimmy, you are one dead fish," I told him.

"You must be Grumpy's sister, Pissy," Jesse fired back.

"Or his cousin, PMSy," chimed in Gabe.

"Zip it, both of you!" I snapped. And then I started thinking, *Why didn't I just ask him to be careful? Why don't I work and play well with others?* I felt a little bad.

"Sorry," I said. "I'm just really hot and not in a good way, and I really want to get to Willard ASAP."

"Us, too, KT," said Gabe. "Hey, look."

Suddenly we began to see some greenery, almost like an oasis in the desert, along with signs marking hiking paths.

"I think I could find a tree there to hide behind while I take a leak," announced Jesse.

"I'm with you conceptually. Different trees, of course," agreed Gabe. "Pull over, KT."

I steered the Jeep onto the shoulder of the road, and the boys hopped out and disappeared. Then I leaned back, closed my eyes, and thought about Willard but I couldn't picture him. So I listened inside of my head really hard, and when I did, I could hear Paul Simon singing "Father and Daughter." He's one of my favorite singer/songwriters from the sixties. He sings so cool and sweet, and the words are so beautiful, I sang a little harmony with him:

"I'm gonna watch you shine
Gonna watch you grow
Gonna paint a sign

So you always know
As long as one and one is two
There could never be a father
Love his daughter more than I love you."

I could almost feel my bio dad's arms around me even though I couldn't see his face. It felt so good, it made me smile, but I felt myself tearing up at the same time. Then I heard Jesse's voice, and I got it together.

"We found a little lake," he told me. "There's nobody around at all. We can wash off this road stink. I brought towels and soap and shampoo."

"Why am I not surprised you'd come equipped with toiletries?" I asked, even though I was glad he did.

He scooped his stuff out of his initialed suitcase, and I followed him down a path. About a quarter of a mile in, I saw a hand-lettered sign with the words Swim At Your Own Risk and an arrow pointing down the path. A minute later, we walked into a little clearing where some scrubby bushes surrounded a greenish-blue pond. Gabe was already floating in it, wearing his shorts and glasses. Jesse took off his T-shirt, and I couldn't help but notice that formidable six-pack all swimmers seem to have before he jumped in. I left my T and shorts on and joined them. We just floated around in the cool water for a while.

"I wonder what my mom and dad are doing now," Gabe asked, half to himself.

"They're probably scarfing down at a buffet table," Jesse said. "Back in the day when we were a family, we cruised in the Bahamas. We each gained five pounds. It was . . ." His voice got a little choked and he tapered off.

"Do your parents go on a lot of cruises?" I asked Gabe, trying to distract Jesse.

"No, they won this trip in a ballroom dancing contest. They were into that stuff way before *Dancing with the Stars*. You should see them. My dad's like this battering ram of an ex-football player, but he's real graceful. And my mom is so tiny, he picks her up and spins her over his head. They're awesome to watch. I would love to have that kind of relationship with someone, but I can't even bring myself to ask anyone out."

"That's usually the first step," I told him. "But don't sweat it, Butchie, that'll change." I paddled around him.

Then I looked at his face and knew this was really painful and serious for him.

"Truth is, Gabriel Butcherelli, I'm a little jealous of you and your parental units."

"They're cool," Gabe said. "But nobody's life is perfect. There's stuff I wish I could change when I'm out in the world."

"Like what?' Jesse asked.

"You know, the girl problem. I know I look kind of nerdy and not in a cool way. Don't tell anyone, but I've never had a date."

"Girls would like you if they got to know you," Jesse said, soaping under his arms. "As long as you lay off the Silver Smoke trick."

"I never get far enough to do any magic tricks," Gabe

answered, missing the soap that was tossed to him.

"If you want a girl, Butchie, my advice would be to lose the magic tricks completely, but still be yourself. Believe me, some girls are looking for Mr. Adorkable," I told him. "They wouldn't be caught dead with Swimmy."

"I wouldn't go that far," Jesse protested.

"Well, here I am," Gabe said, fishing out the soap and flipping it to me. "A geek god. Just send 'em over."

Jesse opened a bottle of some kind of expensive shampoo, lathered his hair, and put the bottle in my outstretched hand. I poured it over my head and rubbed it in.

"Save a little for me," Gabe cautioned.

"Listen, Butcherelli. Since we're related, it's in my interest to give you girl-talk lessons. I don't want you going around embarrassing me," Jesse said. "I've decided to invest some energy into thinking about it." And with that he closed his eyes and floated away still lathered, with bubbles rising all around him.

"He's floating away to fart," I said loud enough for Swimmy to hear me.

Gabe poured on some shampoo and massaged his head. "I like this stuff," he said. "It's very alkaline."

"What's that mean?"

"It makes your hair lighter. In chem class, we found out if you dye your hair with certain dyes, it can take the color out of it."

I swallowed hard and submerged, rubbing my hands through my hair. When I came up for air, there was a circle of dark water around me, and Jesse was back.

"Hey," he smiled at me, "you look better."

"What do you mean?" I panicked.

"Your hair looks different," Gabe observed.

"Oh my god!" I screamed.

I splashed to shore and wrapped one of Jesse's towels around my head.

"We gotta go."

Just then the bushes parted, and two chicks on horses trotted to edge of the pool. They wore bathing suit tops, shorts, boots, and cowboy hats.

"Hi, y'all," said the redhead, scoping out Jesse. "I'm Dene, and this is JoBeth."

JoBeth waved and flashed a toothy smile at the boys, who were treading water. "Mind if I join you?" she asked, pulling off her cowboy hat to release a cascade of dark curls.

"What else are you gonna take off?" Jesse grinned.

"Whatcha got in mind, Blue Eyes?" JoBeth giggled.

"You boys got names?" asked Dene.

"I'm Jesse, and this is Gabe."

"We gotta go, man," said Gabe, getting out of the water.

"Hey, Gabe, whatcha look like without those glasses?" Dene asked.

"I dunno," Gabe answered seriously. "I can't see when I look in the mirror without 'em."

Oh my god, Jesse's lessons for Gabe could not start soon enough.

"Let's go, please," I begged Gabe and Jesse. I was at a stomach-clenching level of anxious. Between Gabe and my hair situation, I was losing whatever cool I had left.

"Well, honey lamb, I think you're cute in a goofy kind of way," Dene giggled.

"C'mon, Jess. KT's losing it. Get moving," Gabe urged.

Jesse rolled his eyes. "Damn," he said, "this was just beginning to get interesting." He climbed out of the water reluctantly and, I might add, slowly. JoBeth and Dene were properly impressed. I could have sworn that even the horses snorted.

"Come on! We're losing time!" I yelled. I wanted to get back to the Jeep and look in the mirror, even though I was scared to see my hair.

"That your girlfriend, Jesse?" JoBeth asked, shooting daggers at me from her eyes.

"No way! That's my, uh, um . . . we're related."

He was still waving at them as Gabe pushed and I pulled him down the path and back to the road.

Gabe, who hadn't had a bad allergy attack all through Texas, began sneezing and spraying again.

"You allergic to girls?" Jesse wanted to know when we reached the car.

Gabe threw him a look that, for Gabe, was a hostile look, but it wouldn't have scared a bunny.

"Absolutely not," he retorted. "I'm just confused. When they're not interested, I get depressed, and when something like what just happened happens, I get scared. I haven't the faintest idea what girls want from me. I gotta figure out how to relate. It's too lonely like this."

And then I screamed so loud that I scared all of us, including me. There in the side-view mirror, I saw my freshly towel-dried hair. It was blah, bland, boring. It was my real color, blond. I looked like . . . how can I say this . . . grotesquely normal. My black hair was gone, my blue streak was gone, my persona was gone—my whole sense of me had been washed away in a New Mexico desert pool by Swimmy's super shampoo. I now looked like, horror of horrors . . . Jesse.

"Oh my god!" I crawled into the back seat with my head in my hands.

"Hey, KT, don't freak. It looks good, really. You look nice," Gabe said softly.

"Nice is the last way I want to look," I growled.

"Please don't be mad at me," Jesse begged. "I didn't know. I use that shampoo all the time."

"I'm sure you do, Blondie," I sniffled.

"I have some disappearing black ink in my magic case. We could pour it on your head," Gabe offered.

"What good is it if it disappears?" snapped Jesse.

"Maybe it won't disappear on hair," Gabe whispered hopefully.

"I feel naked and wrong. Don't look at me," I said. "Let's just go."

"Let's take our chances on the interstate," Jesse whispered to Gabe. "We gotta make something good happen for her, fast."

I pulled the door closed, lay down on the seat next to my guitar, and threw my sweatshirt over my head. I was horrified, but way down deep, though I would never admit it, I really felt it was very cool and kind of reassuring to look like someone I knew.

"Wake me up when we get to Sedona," I told them.

Then, like someone in shock, which I was, I passed out.

chapter sixteen

When I woke up, we had reached Sedona for sure. The sky was turning pink and orange, and the strange red rock formations looked just like the ones I'd seen in pictures. There were castles and rabbit ears and Snoopy, and even a few that looked like body parts. The whole landscape had a funny kind of otherworldly feeling to it, like we'd entered some kind of parallel universe. I took a peek in the mirror. Unfortunately my hair looked like crap in this universe, too.

"Next right is Mountain Road, Gabe," Jesse said as he traced our progress on a map.

I sat up, ran my fingers through the stuff on my head, and tried not to think about my follicles. I didn't want anything to spoil the moment that was waiting for me, the moment of meeting my bio dad, the real one.

The route kept winding, taking us higher up into the mountains. The dust swirled around the Jeep as we bumped along the unpaved road. There were no houses along the way, just rocks and trees and some places where bunches of daisies grew out of the dirt alongside the road. I thought they looked like hope would look if it were a flower.

"Whoa, Gabe, slow down!" Jesse ordered, and I felt my heart beating double time. There was a sign up ahead, and as we drew closer, we could see it: PINCHEKUS CERTIFIED HYPNOTHERAPY AND FAMILY COUNSELING – 2 MILES. We exploded with cheers, and Gabe pressed down on the accelerator.

In a little while, we slowed to read another sign: HEADACHES? LICENSED KINESIOLOGIST 1.8 MILES. We cheered again. Then another: REGISTERED TATTOO ARTIST AND CONFIDENTIAL BODY PIERCING BY WILLARD – 1/2 MILE. We cheered a little half-heartedly.

"That's probably just a hobby," Gabe said.

"Sure," I agreed. "He's an artist."

"Let's hope so," said Jesse.

Then: ACCREDITED AIR DUCT CLEANING 500 YARDS. Our cheer was kind of feeble this time. It faded completely at MEDICAL COLONICS and then exploded when we saw the lettering under it: NOT HERE. 5 MILES BACK ON RED ROCK ROAD.

"Gabe, stop for a minute," I said.

Gabe pulled to the side of the winding dirt road.

"You look fine," he said. "Believe me."

"It's not that," I told him. "I want to remember this moment and how it feels. It's my last moment of not knowing who I really am. After today, that empty place inside me is gonna be filled in and filled up. I'm going to make sense to myself and to the world."

"It can only be an improvement," cracked Jesse.

"Shut it down, man," Gabe reprimanded him. "She's right. We should do something like drink a toast."

"My bad," admitted Jesse, pulling a water bottle from the cup holder. "Here's to 908—to Willard, our dad. Pinchekus kids rule!" He took a swig and passed it to Gabe. Gabe gulped and handed it me. I took it and finished off the bottle.

"I'm ready now," I said. "Let's go, boys."

⁂

We pulled into a dirt parking area at the top of the mountain next to a three-wheeled car that had what looked like homemade solar panels attached to the roof. We got out of the Jeep in slow motion, or at least it felt like slow motion. We looked up and our mouths fell open. In front of us, a white pyramid rose from the desert floor. Whirligigs lined the path leading to it, and goats, chickens, and baby pigs wandered around. We stood there speechless.

"I guess King Tut found the simple life," Gabe breathed.

"Whoever he is, he's our dad, so don't make fun," I told him.

"Check this out," Jesse laughed. A piglet was rubbing against his leg and looking up at him adoringly. Jesse picked it up and scratched it behind its ear. The minute he put it down, the little porker began to squeal. "I guess he's coming with us," Swimmy said. He picked up the baby pig, which promptly began licking his face.

As we headed up the path, a large tattooed woman stepped out from behind a boulder. We all jumped. She was wearing one Ugg boot and struggling to hold onto a large snake with a huge lump in its middle.

"Oh my goodness," she said. "You almost made me drop Luna."

"Please don't do that," I pleaded.

"She is a little cranky," admitted the woman. "We're going to the vet. That's what we get for eating my Uggs," she said to the snake. "A big tummy ache." She smiled at us. "I'm Aurora. Go on up. Willard's expecting you."

"But he doesn't know we're coming," Gabe asserted. "How could he be expecting us?"

Aurora headed for the little car. "He knows everything," she threw over her shoulder. "He has a psychic degree from Horvard."

As she zipped out of her parking spot, we walked up the path and then onto an adjoining ramp leading to the pyramid entrance. At the open door stood a shadowed figure, arms extended in welcome. As we got closer, we could see that he was wiry, barefoot, and wearing faded cutoff jeans. He looked to be in his late thirties, about the age of all my mom's boyfriends, but his head was bald and shiny.

"I'm Willard," he said, smiling. "And I know you're not here for tattoos."

"Maybe one that says 'Dad,'" I choked out, holding back all the stuff that was welling up in me.

"In a heart, of course." He smiled, turned, and walked back into the house. We followed him into a big room with pillows strewn across the stone floor. Jesse was still carrying the piglet.

In one corner was a dental-type chair facing a huge window. Next to it was a table with a tattoo gun, disposable gloves, and dyes. A deck jutted out into space, facing the red rock mountains. Willard walked toward the chair and we trailed him, all talking at once.

"You gotta tell me," Jesse implored. "Do you shave your head or am I gonna be bald?"

"Did you build this place? Do you know anything about magic?" Gabe wanted to know.

"Are you musical? Were you ever in a bad mood for, like, years?" I asked.

"We're 908 sperm donor kids," Gabe finally announced.

Willard climbed into the chair and swiveled to face us. He nodded and smiled.

"I know," he said. "I've been waiting for you."

chapter seventeen

"Aurora made lemonade for you this morning. Of course she's made it for the past three mornings. Sometimes my estimated times of arrival are a little off."

Willard pointed to a stool with a tray, a pitcher, and three glasses. "Help yourselves."

We poured our drinks in silence as the sun slowly disappeared into the mountains behind our biological father's gleaming dome. The piglet followed Jesse and crawled into his lap when we sat down on the floor cushions at Willard's feet.

"I'm KT," I said, looking up at him. For the first time in my life, I felt kind of timid.

"Of course you are," he smiled.

"I'm Jesse. Please, I need the 411 on the hair situation, ASAP."

"It will be revealed," Willard answered. "And you are?"

"I'm Gabe."

"Well, Gabe, Jesse, and KT, I'm sure you want to know everything from the beginning."

"Every single detail," I said. I was feeling all emotional and weepy at the thought of hearing the story of my own creation.

"And you shall. You must," Willard continued. He settled back and closed his eyes as if to picture the past in perfect detail, and then he began. "The day I went to Cryosperm was miraculous. The moon was in Aquarius, and it also happened to be garbage day. My tuition check to Horvard had bounced, and I was desperate to continue my Samoan language studies. Cryosperm had accepted my application, and they paid fifty dollars, a princely sum for someone of my limited means. I was also uplifted by the idea that my seed would be put to such good use. I felt sure that my profile would be chosen since at that point in time, I resembled a young Kurt Cobain."

"Then you did have hair. What happened?" Jesse's voice was intense.

"Patience, Jesse," Willard answered. He steepled his hands as if praying for guidance and went on. "I used a Walkman in my linguistic curriculum, and I was strolling to Cryosperm, deeply engrossed in conjugating the verb *alofa,* meaning 'to love,' when I reached the edge of the sidewalk opposite my destination. I could have sworn the sign blinked 'WALK' so I stepped off the curb. Because of my earphones, I was unaware that a nearby garbage truck was loading trash-cans. Across the street, although I did not know it then, my beautiful Aurora was ready to cross as she sipped a large Slurpee. I didn't hear either the garbage truck or the approaching motorcycle. Nor did I see a piece of watermelon rind escape from a trashcan and roll into the street, although later Aurora told me that's what occurred. I happened to look up in time to see Aurora frantically signaling danger approaching, but I had no time to react. By the time I turned to see the oncoming Harley motorcycle, it had already skidded on the rind and crashed, into . . . my crotch."

"Ouch," Jesse and Gabe gasped.

"An understatement," Willard responded. "The motorcyclist, who was about my age, weight, and height, with blond hair like mine, jumped off the bike and kneeled over me. I could see the concern in his blue eyes. Then he spoke. 'Holy shit, man,' he exclaimed. 'You're okay, right?'"

"'Not okay,'" I gasped. At that point Aurora had reached my side. She kneeled beside me and dumped her Slurpee on my crotch. 'You need to ice it,' she said. Then she and the biker helped me to the curb. Even in my agony, I was hypnotized by Aurora."

"It's a wonder we're not all deformed after that," Jesse observed.

Willard ignored him and continued. "The biker felt my pain, and I could feel his sincerity. 'Oh man, I'm so sorry. How can I help you? What can I do?' he asked. I tore my eyes from Aurora and removed an envelope containing my accepted Cryosperm application from my jacket pocket. 'Take this,' I told him. 'Be me for one exquisite minute and get me my fifty bucks.'

"He nodded, grasped my hand in some sort of strange biker handshake that implied solidarity, and took the envelope. Shortly afterward, he returned with my money and another apology. Then he got on his bike and rode off. I never saw him again."

There was a long moment as we all took in what he had just told us. "Then you're not our bio dad," I whispered finally. My eyes welled up and big, fat tears rolled down my cheeks. I had never felt such an enormous sense of emptiness. My whole being, every part of me, felt impossibly sad and wounded, like my soul was dying.

"You're not our dad," I repeated hoarsely.

"I'm afraid not," Willard admitted. "The biker gave his seed with my profile. It was a sad day for me, as well—I so wanted to contribute. But on that day, I did meet Aurora, the love of my life."

"Why didn't you ask the guy his name?" I demanded.

"Perhaps I should have, KT, but I was in agony and besotted with love."

"So your hair situation has nothing to do with me," Jesse observed, stating the obvious as usual.

"No, but I am quite hirsute. My head is shaved by Aurora twice weekly."

"So all we know is that he rides a Harley and plays the guitar. That sure narrows it down," I barked.

I felt so incredibly terrible, it was hard for me to speak in a normal voice.

"I'm sorry you didn't find your answer," Willard said, "but you will. I'm sure of it. This house is built on a vortex. There is great spiritual energy here that facilitates healing."

"Yeah, I'll bet," I mumbled.

"Have you ever considered the serendipitous synchronicity involved in all of you posting on the Internet at approximately the same time?" Willard asked.

"What does that mean?" Jesse asked Gabe.

"It means that our finding each other was more than coincidence," Gabe answered.

"How did you know about that?" Jesse asked Willard.

"I know things because I'm in tune with the universe and, of course, because of my studies at Horvard. I know that you were meant to find each other, and so you did."

"Our finding each other doesn't mean anything if we don't find our bio dad," I blurted out, and I saw a hurt look flash across Gabe's face.

"This is a full-blown, total disaster," Jesse added. "What am I gonna do now? Where am I gonna live?"

"You will all find what you are seeking," Willard insisted. "I'm sure of it. I'm psychic, you know."

"I am, too," I said. "And I see us leaving."

"Why don't you and Gabe finish your lemonade while Jesse and I spend some time together? You'll need to wear these," he told Jesse, handing him some hemp sandals. "Your feet affect your soul, you know, and your soul affects your head."

"And your shinbone's connected to your knee bone," I whispered, mocking him. I was still in pain but I rolled my eyes, and Jesse stifled a laugh as he took off his Chucks. I was going into numbness mode, when something hurts so much that you just shut down.

"I'm with you," he said as Willard put a hand on his shoulder and guided him and the piglet out onto the deck and down the stairs. Swimmy looked back at us with an eye roll of his own.

Gabe and I followed them onto the balcony. We stood at the rail, watching as they began to walk the concentric circles of a stone labyrinth in the center of a desert garden. As they wandered the maze, lit only by a full moon and the sparkling stars of the Sedona sky, they became more and more engrossed in conversation. The piglet trailed Jesse, who actually seemed to be interested in what Willard was saying.

"Why do you think he asked Jesse to walk with him?" Gabe asked.

"Maybe because Jesse's highest on the jerkometer," I answered.

Gabe finished off his lemonade and set the glass down on a nearby table. "I wouldn't jump to that conclusion," he said.

We stood there in silence as Willard handed Jesse something. They both kneeled as Jesse threw some stones on the path.

"What bullshit thing are they doing now?" I asked.

"That's called throwing the runes," Gabe answered patiently. "The runes are special stones, and some people believe you can use them to gain spiritual insights."

"Some people are idiots, and the rest are pains in the ass."

"What are you so mad at, KT?" Gabe asked me softly.

"Why do you care?" I wanted to know.

"'Cause you're my sister, and in my family, people care about each other and the way they feel."

"In my family," I told him, "people make lousy decisions and nobody sticks around. I have never in my entire life seen a relationship between a man and a woman that's worked out. It's been my experience that they always turn to crap."

"I get it now," he responded. "That would piss me off, too."

Our eyes locked, and when I looked at him it was as if I was seeing him, really seeing him, for the first time. I knew exactly who he was, and I knew he knew exactly who I was. That scared me a little, but it felt kind of good at the same time.

"Besides," I continued, ignoring the good feeling, "rock and roll is rebellious. Being pissed off is good for my writing."

"That's what you say to make it okay," he said gently. "What you told me before is the real reason." He reached out as if he was going to hug me, and then he sneezed, snuffled, and blew his nose in a tiny scrap of a used tissue.

"Do pigs shed?" he asked.

The old Gabe was back, but it struck me that maybe the other one was there all the time, as well. "All these farm animals are going to kill me," he said so seriously that I laughed until I almost peed. He didn't seem to mind. As a matter of fact, soon we both were rocking back and forth with laughter, and then we did hug, and it felt surprisingly good.

chapter eighteen

Willard and the piglet walked us all to the parking area. By that time, Gabe was shooting allergy spray and snuffling like a walrus.

"Sorry you can't stay for dinner," Willard told us. "I wanted you to get to know Aurora, but I am positive that this is the absolute right moment for you to leave."

"Me, too," Gabe sneezed. "I don't want to be rude, but I think your barnyard friends have a contract out on me."

Willard hugged him and reached over to hug me. I couldn't do the hugging thing, especially with the guy who screwed up getting our dad's name. He instinctively pulled back.

"Stay hopeful, KT," he said.

"It's not my style," I told him and slid behind the wheel.

"I enjoyed our talk," he said to Jesse. "You're an excellent student." They did the man hug, back-patting thing.

"Thank you for my shoes and for everything you shared. This was a very important day for me." Jesse picked up the baby pig, smooched it on the snout, and handed it to Willard. It was a truly bizarre thing for Bacon Boy to do. "I'll never forget you," he said to the pig. Then he added mysteriously, "Nothing with a face," and he and Willard smiled at each other.

"There's a cantina up the main road if you're hungry," Willard suggested. "As a matter of fact, my Horvard training is telling me it's very important that you go there, and strangely enough, it's telling me to advise you to watch the TV."

"I hate Mexican food and TV," I countered, pulling out the car and pointing it away from the scene of our disappointment.

"Give it a chance, KT," Willard called after us. "I swear to you, it will all work out."

I watched him wave goodbye in the rearview mirror, his silly head gleaming in the moonlight as we disappeared into the dust, heading back to civilization.

You'd think that Gabe and I would have jumped on Jesse, wanting to find out everything that went on between him and Willard, but our situation had, somehow, just begun to sink in. We were all digesting the fact that we had no biological dad, no plan, and nowhere to go but home. We'd reached the end of our search. It sucked beyond words, and nobody said a thing until we rolled into the parking lot of the Red Rock Cantina. It was filled with old cars and battered pickups, and the Jeep fit right in. A neon sign on the cantina flashed:

COCKTAILS-BEER-DANCING-FOOD.

Underneath it, another sign read:

TONIGHT IN PERSON: THE MOTHER TRUCKERS.

Country music drifted through the desert night.

As we walked to the door, Jesse finally spoke. His profound words were, "Do you think there's line dancing?"

"Are you asking like that would be a good thing?" I said. "I can assure you if there is, we're leaving."

"We'll take a vote," Gabe informed me. I rolled my eyes at him in return. A vote was not happening.

We opened the door to a sawdust-on-the-floor kind of joint with tables, booths, a small stage, a bar with a TV set, and about twenty customers, most of them cowboy types.

When we stepped through the door, it was kind of dark and some cowboy carded us. Then he stamped our hands so that no one could serve us beer.

Onstage, The Mother Truckers were winding up a song to applause. As we stood in the darkened entry, the lead singer made an announcement.

"Hey, everybody! I want y'all to meet The Mother Truckers' new pal, who kept us company all the way from Joplin. It was better than a case of Red Bull, listening to his songs about his love for KT, the little ladybug who's been makin' his life a livin' hell. Give it up for Dylan Stewart."

And there he was under a single spot on stage . . . puppy boy. I thought I would freak out on the spot, but I bit my lip and held it together. Then he began to sing, "Nobody Loves You Like Me," one of the zillion songs he's written about me. Even in my depressed, flipped out, hopeless, screwed-up, dead-tired, bummed-out state, I noticed two shocking things I had never noticed before: Dylan could really sing and Dylan looked really hot. His dark hair was all messy, but in a good way. His big, brown eyes were really intense, and when he played guitar, the muscles in his arms rippled. This puppy was a contender for best in show. Why had I never seen that before? Then I came to, remembered what had just happened, and he became old annoying Dylan again.

"That's a pretty song," Jesse said. "You really know that dude?"

I turned to head out the door, but Gabe grabbed my arm.

"Please, KT," he whispered. "Go with the flow for once."

What could I do? We walked into the light of the restaurant, and Dylan stopped singing.

"This is her," he announced into the mike. "I can't believe it! It's my girl, KT, in person. She's walking into this cantina and back into my life."

The whole place turned to give me the stink eye. There were a few hisses and a couple of boos.

"Don't be hard on her," Dylan told them. "I love her."

They only hissed louder, so he started singing again as we slid into a booth, and I tried to disappear. He finished the song to huge applause and sneaked off the stage as The Mother Truckers ended their set. Then he walked over to where we were sitting.

"Hey, man," Jesse said, "I liked your song."

"Thanks," he said, looking only at me.

"You can sit down, Dylan," I told him.

"This is amazing. You look beautiful with that color hair," he said. "I was going to start looking for you tomorrow."

"My heartfelt congrats. You're ahead of schedule."

The waitress, who looked about our age, came over to the table.

"My name is Daisy, and I'll be your server," she announced. "Your song was bitchin', Dylan." Then she smiled a dazzling smile that seemed to be directed at Gabe. "You guys decided on your order?"

We told her what we wanted, and she walked away humming "Nobody Loves You Like Me."

Then Jesse and Gabe jumped in, asking Dylan all kinds of questions about his travels with The Mother Truckers. I was relieved that I didn't have to talk.

When Daisy came back, she set Dylan's order of tamales down in front of him. "It's on the house, Dylan," she said. She slid Jesse's plate over to him. "One vegetarian special." Then she served Gabe. "Chile relleno . . . very hot," she said pointedly, smiling, "for . . .?"

"Gabe," he prompted her. He smiled back, and if

they had been in a comic book, there would have been little hearts in the balloons over their heads.

"*Arroz con* whatever for you, KT. I think the chef spit in it." And then she plunked my plate down hard in front of me. "Enjoy."

I turned to Dylan. "We're not meant to be, Dylan," I told him wearily.

"You're wrong, KT," he answered softly. "I'd be really good for you."

I wanted to cry for so many reasons. "Please," I breathed, "I can't do this. Especially now." I picked up my plate and walked over to the empty bar. I needed to be alone.

As I walked away, I could hear Dylan asking if we'd met our bio dad yet and Gabe telling him the reason I was so bummed was that Willard had turned out not to be our dad. Then I noticed Daisy sliding into the seat next to Gabe, saying, "Can I hang out with you on my break?"

It looked like Abracadabra was feeling the magic instead of making it. He took off his glasses, and his face lit up with a big grin that actually made him look kind of cute. I could see Daisy chatting away, and he was getting into the conversation thing without any lessons from Jesse.

I looked up at the TV. It was tuned to *David Letterman*, and Dave was saying, "And now we're back with Jimmy Savage, certified maniac and former lead singer of Bad Angels."

The dude who was sitting in the guest seat was wearing skintight leather pants, cowboy boots, a purple plaid shirt, and an orange patterned bandana on his head. He smiled and waved at the camera.

"It's been said," Letterman told him, "that if Axl Rose and Bruce Springsteen had a baby, Jimmy, it would have been you."

"I've heard that, Dave," the dude answered. "And I've addressed it in a song on my new solo album that's called 'The Boss, the Madman, and Me.'"

There was scattered applause from the audience.

"I guess not everyone's heard it yet, or maybe they have," said Dave. There were a few scattered chuckles. "You look like you were born to be a rock star, Jimmy. You ever do anything else?"

"I went into the nonprofit field right out of high school."

"What did you do?"

"I put together a band."

It took Dave and the audience a second to get it, and Paul Shaffer, the bandleader and keyboard player, yelled, "Musicians don't make money at first."

"Ah. I get it," Dave explained. The audience chuckled appreciatively. "But I understand you've had some other unusual gigs."

"Right! The best one I ever had was selling my sperm in St. Louis back in the nineties. Very cool."

The audience laughed, they were really interested now, and I called to Gabe and Jesse. "Hey, c'mere, quick!" They joined me at the bar, with Dylan and Daisy tagging along. "Get a load of this dude," I said.

"Tell us more," Letterman encouraged him. "This is a subject of great interest. Did you have to audition or do they accept just anyone?"

"I didn't have to audition although I would have been happy to," Jimmy answered, smiling. The audience was warming toward him. This was the good stuff.

"So where did you go to make this donation?" Dave inquired.

"Well, the place was called Cryosperm. It was in St. Louis. Early '90s, I believe. I even memorialized my donation. Check this out." Jimmy rolled up his sleeve and searched through the snakes and dragons on his arm. When he found what he was looking for, we all gasped and even clutched each other's arms. It was a moment that could only be described as cosmic, soul shaking, magnificent, and beyond belief . . . because there on Jimmy Savage's arm was a big beautiful tattoo: DONOR 908.

We stood there, frozen and speechless.

"Did you do it just for the fun or was there big money in that?" Dave quipped.

"Fifty bucks, Dave. Big money in the day, but I gave it to a friend."

The audience applauded. They were loving him now, and he was loving them loving him, as was Dave.

"So," asked Dave, milking it, "you think there's any little Jimmys running around?"

Jimmy stood up, faced the camera, and held out his arms, offering himself to his fans, "You tell me, ladies. Anybody out there as good looking as me?"

The audience went wild, and so did we. I started screaming, "It's him! It's our bio dad!" and jumping up and down like a head case.

"I can't believe our bio dad's a rock star," Gabe whispered, in shock. "I was a 'listener' in chorus."

"Oh my god! So was I!" squealed Daisy.

"I do kind of look like him," Jesse said, moving closer to the TV.

"I knew you were special, KT," Dylan told me.

I shushed them as the audience settled down. Everyone was glued to the screen as Dave continued.

"And your selflessness continues. I hear that tomorrow you're playing in the First Annual Celebrity Golf Classic at the L.A. Country Club to benefit . . ." He looked closer at the card he was reading. "CVD. Do you really have Cardio Vascular Disease? We have to talk. You know I had a quintuple bypass."

"Yes, I know, Dave," Jimmy returned. "But in this case, CVD stands for Color Vision Deficiency, otherwise known as color blindness."

Dave did a double take that got a laugh. "Color blindness. Was ingrown toenail taken?"

"It's my disease, Dave," Jimmy replied sincerely. "I know personally that CVD can lead to severe depression and lack of self-esteem."

"And outfits like yours." Dave held up Jimmy's record as the theme music began to play. "Jimmy Savage, *adios*, Ladies and Gentlemen! Good night!"

We all started high-fiving and jumping for joy. I had

gone from the deepest depths to the highest high of my life in just a few minutes. For a millisecond, I thought about Willard telling me to stay hopeful, and how, if we hadn't gone to see him when we did and left at the exact time we did, we never would have been at the cantina to see the Letterman show. I wondered if maybe things did happen for a reason.

Then I heard Gabe saying to Daisy, "Do you think you could get us some cans of caffeine? Pulse, Jolt, Red Bull, whatever you've got. We're leaving for L.A. now!" and I saw our teen waitress scurrying off to the kitchen.

I noticed that Dylan had walked to the side of the stage to pick up his guitar, and I went over to him.

"I know what this means to you," he said tenderly.

"I know you do," I told him. "So go home now, Dylan, and please, just let me do what I have to do." And with that, I headed for the ladies' room to get in a final pee and make room for the caffeine. As I walked down the hall, I heard Jesse talking to Dylan, so I stopped for a second to listen.

"Hey, Dylan," said Jesse, "you okay?"

"I really love her." Dylan's voice cracked a little bit.

"I feel you, man. I really do."

"So please, take good care of her," Dylan instructed him.

I couldn't take any more. I suddenly began feeling guilty. It was so annoying. I had never asked him to fall in love with me. To tell the truth, I had never felt I was very lovable. But here he was, in pain on account of me, and I was feeling bad about it. I had never felt guilty about it before. Something inside me seemed to be shifting. I didn't know what was happening, but I knew it was annoying. I'd had enough. I ran into the ladies' room, and when I came out, Dylan was gone.

Jesse and Gabe were standing at the bar waiting for the drinks.

"It's mind-blowing," Jesse said. "We're actually members of the Lucky Sperm Club."

"What's that?" Gabe wanted to know.

"In the beginning it meant kids who were lucky enough to have rich parents, but now it includes the kids of celebrities," I told them. "It means anyone who has good stuff happening just because they are who they are. And we're the Savages." When we realized what I had just said, we all burst out laughing.

"And I can get a tattoo," I added. "Maybe on the way home, we can stop off at Willard's."

"This is so crazy," Gabe said.

Jesse looked down at his hemp shoes. "Willard told me the path would be revealed. And he said that we were on a journey to find something more than our dad. I better go out to the car and make room." With that, he headed out the door.

Gabe and I stood there puzzled. "What do you mean by 'make room'? For what?" I called after Jesse.

Just then, Daisy arrived with a huge bag of canned drinks. The way she smiled at Gabe told me that I should get lost, but I really wanted to know what was happening, so I moved off a little way, but still within earshot. They didn't know or care where I was.

"You think this is enough?" Daisy asked.

"It's perfect," Gabe said, taking the bag from her. "Hey, can you tell me how come you're so nice and easy to talk to?"

"I don't know," Daisy answered. "When you figure it out, you tell me."

"I will," Gabe said, looking into her eyes. "You know, you look a lot like Miley Cyrus, but prettier."

"Everybody tells me that," Daisy giggled.

"But much prettier," he added shyly.

They stood there just smiling at each other. It was sweet and revolting at the same time.

"Hey, Gabe," Daisy asked finally, "do you think you could make room for me in your car?"

chapter nineteen

There was nothing I could do. She attached herself to Gabe and there was no saying no. Strangely, by the time we got to the car, Jesse had already taken off the top and rearranged all our stuff so there was a little more room in the back seat. How did he know we would need it? I don't know. Something had happened to him in that labyrinth, and he was tuned into everything on another level. Except for the line-dancing remark, Swimmy seemed like a different person. I kind of missed the old, self-involved dude I was used to. He was waiting at the wheel, and I got in the shotgun seat while Gabe and Daisy squeezed into the back.

Jesse turned on a soft-rock station that made me nauseous, but I knew enough not to say anything. We took off into the warm, starry desert night and I pretended to be asleep while I listened to the conversation behind me. This is how it went:

DAISY: So after a gazillion people told me I looked like Miley, I knew what I was meant to do.

GABE: Be a singer?

DAISY: Wrong. I told you I can't sing.

GABE: Be a movie star?

DAISY: No, silly, I can't act to save my life.

GABE: Then what?

DAISY: What I was meant to do is to be Miley Cyrus's stand-in. That's the person they focus the lights on. And sometimes that person gets to hang out with the star. I've made a study of it.

GABE: You're very determined, aren't you?

DAISY: I am, and when you said you were driving to L.A., I knew it was a sign for me to go for my dream. Do you have a dream, Gabe?

I'd never heard anything quite like this before. My *arroz* rose in my throat. This kind of talk was truly puke-worthy. I looked at Jesse, who was speeding and swigging a can of Jolt. He was smiling. I could see we were not at all on the same page, so I decided to go to sleep to escape the horror of what was going on around me.

As I dropped off, I could hear Gabe saying, "I think I want to be a scientist or a magician, but I haven't decided yet."

And Daisy cooing, "Whatever you do, you're going to stand out. You're so different."

And Gabe answering, "You're different, too. You're the first girl I've ever felt comfortable with."

"You're just sayin' that."

"No, I'm not. I always say exactly what I mean except when I'm doing magic."

"Me, too," Daisy answered.

Thankfully, at that point I went unconscious. When I woke up, Daisy was giving herself a manicure, and we were just passing through Victorville. I checked the gas gauge, which was dangerously close to empty.

"We're gonna need gas soon," I announced. We had enough gas money to get us to L.A., but I wanted to see where she was coming from. "You kicking in, Daisy?

"Of course I am," she declared. "My granddaddy used to live in Victorville, so I know this area. There's a little casino with a pump about forty miles up the road. Do you think we can make it forty miles on what we got?"

"If we're lucky," I snapped. Why did I find everything she said annoying?

"What do you think, Gabe?" she asked. "Do you feel lucky?" "Very," he told her.

I turned around so if I did puke, it would be on them. Then I had to watch as she took Gabe's hand in hers.

"I bet you never had a manicure," she said softly. "I'd like to give you your first." And that's what she proceeded to do. Really. She actually pulled out a manicure kit and filed and shaped his nails, massaged his hands with lotion, and applied clear polish with the greatest of care, after which she fell asleep with her head on his shoulder. And he just sat there, with his eyes wide open and a dopey smile on his face, checking out his hands and drinking up her closeness.

I opened my mouth to make a bitchy remark. But before I could, Jesse whispered, "Don't spoil it for him, KT. Keep it to yourself." So that's what I did, against my better judgment.

chapter twenty

It was four thirty in the morning, and we were on empty when we saw a huge sign lighting up the night that read GOLDEN NUGGET CASINO. Shiny gold nuggets and sparkling glasses of champagne shooting off neon bubbles surrounded the name, and it stood next to a small motel that featured a lighted swimming pool and a big, slick-looking casino.

Daisy was right. They did have a two-pump gas station. The only trouble was a sign taped to the pump that read WILL OPEN AT 6:00 A.M. We stared at it as if that would change what it said, and when it didn't, we all got out of the car.

"Casino's open," Jesse said. "Think they'd let me play a machine, Daisy?"

"How 'bout me?" I added. "I just chugged a can of Red Bull."

"You can play here at any age and in any condition," quipped Daisy. "You're gonna see a bunch of seniors and probably some toddlers in their mamas' laps. Here, take my tips and win something."

She pulled a handful of change and few crumpled dollar bills out of her purse and handed half to Jesse and half to me.

As we pocketed the money and took off, we saw the lovebirds holding hands and settling into two lounge chairs by the pool.

"Wait a sec, Jess," I said, pretending to tie my shoe. I was feeling really protective about Gabe, and I wanted to hear what was going on. I didn't trust Daisy, and I was scared that she was going to hurt him.

"So many stars," he was saying. "That's the best part about the desert."

Daisy pointed up at the sky. "That one is Miley, and that one's Demi Lovato, and . . ." I looked at Jesse and rolled my eyes. He put his finger to his lips to signal me to hush.

Gabe took her hand and pointed to the brightest star.

"That's the one the light is focused on. That's you, Daisy," he said.

She smiled at him sweetly. I started to go back, but Jesse grabbed my arm and pulled me toward the casino. I could still hear her saying, "You know, it won't be easy saying good-bye to you."

I turned back to hear him say, "We've still got tomorrow." They both lay there with their eyes closed, swinging their clasped hands.

"I have to save him," I told Jesse.

"You have to butt out," he stated gently but emphatically and dragged me toward the casino.

When we walked through the doors, I was amazed to see:

a) how big the place was (probably three hundred slots and fifty gaming tables);
b) how old the patrons were (I guess old people have insomnia, because they were out in force, leaning over the slots with their oxygen tanks next to them like service animals); and
c) how no one checked our IDs or even looked at us sideways.

We decided to play twenty-five cent video poker. I played and Jesse managed to score some free little cheese tarts and Cokes for us from one of the cute waitresses wandering around. We traded off, feeding the machine with no results until suddenly, when we were down to our last few quarters, I put one in and we heard a loud click. A red light began flashing, and the machine started to make crazy noises. We were staring at a straight flush and a sign above the machine was blinking "$300." Then the machine began playing music, and we began hugging each other and jumping up and down. A few of the oldsters turned to stare at us, but most never even looked our way.

We heard a clanking sound and waited for the slot to spit out chips, but nothing happened. "That sounds like money's coming!" Jesse crowed. Still, nothing happened. "Give it up for Mama," I shouted, banging the machine. There was just silence, and then the click of a ticket spitting out above a little sign: YOU MUST BE 21 TO REDEEM WINNING TICKETS.

"We're screwed," I said.

"Whatever it is, KT, it is," Jesse remarked calmly, and with that he headed back to the pool.

I followed him. What the hell had happened to him? When we reached the pool, I pulled a lounge chair closer to Daisy, making as much noise as possible and waking her, which was the point.

Jesse flopped down on a chair near Gabe, who was snoring like an asthmatic warthog.

"Sometimes not getting what you want is getting what you need, and I need sleep." And with that, Jesse closed his eyes and was out.

"Daisy," I asked, "you wouldn't happen to be twenty-one, would you?"

"Uh-uh," she answered, yawning.

I pulled out the ticket and studied it. "Worthless," I said. Daisy took it from my hand and looked it over.

"I can look very mature," she told me, unbuttoning a button on her blouse and pursing her lips in what she thought was a sexy expression.

"You look like a fish with a rack," I said.

"I also have a fake ID," she smiled.

"Go for it, my friend. Three hundred smackeroos, and we'll cut you in."

She kissed Gabe on the forehead, grabbed her backpack, and headed for the casino. I lay back and waited. The Red Bull must have worn off because, in less than five minutes, I was out.

We woke up with sun blazing down on the three of us and a man's voice calling, "If that's your car, either move it or fill it up."

I pried my eyes open to see the gas station attendant hanging an Open sign. Jesse got up, digging for the keys in his jeans.

"Where's Daisy?" asked Gabe.

"She had a fake ID, so she went in to cash our $300 winning ticket," I told him.

Jesse checked his watch. "That was two hours ago."

We all looked around, but we already knew. The only movement we could see was a plastic cup with a straw threaded through a paper sail with Gabe's name on it, floating in the pool. He kneeled, plucked it from the water, read it, put it back in, and watched it float away. "Let's go," he said.

Jesse put his hand on Gabe's shoulder, and they walked toward the Jeep. I hung back. The cup was spinning around in the water, so I got down on my knees to read the message. It read, "It's too hard to say goodbye. Look for me in the stars. Love, Daisy."

chapter twenty-one

I wanted to tell Gabe I had a feeling that Daisy was trouble from the minute she slammed my plate down at the cantina, but something told me not to say a word. *I guess,* I thought, *this is how other people's brains connect to their mouths. They actually think before they speak.* Gabe took the wheel. The backseat probably held too many memories. Jesse and I didn't say anything because there was nothing we could say that could make Gabe feel better.

Jesse waited an hour before reminding us that we needed to come up with a plan to get to Jimmy Savage at the golf tournament. There was sure to be celebrity security, and nobody would ever believe our story. We put our heads together and came up with a simple, but brilliant operation. Gabe actually came out of himself and got involved in cooking up the scheme, and Jesse's shoes had apparently raised his IQ substantially because he invented some of the best elements. I was kind of the overall mastermind, and all together "The Savages" made a pretty good team.

We drove into the parking lot of the L.A. Country Club about a half hour before the tournament was scheduled to begin. There was a huge banner with the words COLOR VISION DEFICIENCY CELEBRITY GOLF TOURNAMENT written on it. A guard at the lot waved us in. It was already more than half full with cars packed in really tight. We got out, took our parking ticket, and gave him our keys. Gabe quickly put on Jesse's purple shorts and my stretched-out lime T-shirt. We reviewed our M.O. and walked to the entrance of the club, where tables were set up for check-in. Color-challenged kids, wearing all sorts of hideous combinations, were wandering around. Gabe fit right in.

We checked out the manicured grounds and the huge, tile-roofed clubhouse, looking for the caddy shack. When we found it, we noticed the "shack" could have housed an army of caddies. I stuffed some lawn clippings from a grounds container into my pocket just as a caddy, about our age, came out of the shack. He was wearing a baseball cap with MARIO LOPEZ written on it. Then a second caddy with a DAVID SPADE cap passed us, and finally came a smirky looking dude wearing a Jimmy Savage cap.

Gabe gave me a nudge. "There's your pigeon."

"Operation Father's Day is underway," I whispered.

I wandered up to Jimmy's caddy, who was locking the door to the shack.

"Cool hat," I told him, smiling. "You really his caddy?"

"Yeah, I'm his guy," he told me. "Only the top caddies get the rock stars."

Once again, my brain actually connected to my mouth. "You must be the best," I cooed.

"I make 'em look good," he said like a true a-hole.

"I bet," I said. Then, in a sexy whisper, I added the capper, "How'd you like to smoke a J?"

"Sweet," he answered. "I just had my drug test."

He set his clubs down and unlocked the door to the shack, and I slithered past him. He followed and closed the door. Then he put his keys down, reached under a pile of towels, and pulled out a booklet of Zig Zags. I took one, rolled the lawn clippings into a J, and handed it to him. He held a match to it, closed his eyes, and took a deep drag.

"This is one fine J," he said, leaning in toward me and trying to look sexy. Actually, he looked dumb and disgusting.

I moved toward him as if to lock lips, grabbed his hat and his keys, and was out the door before he could exhale. I locked it from the outside and handed the baseball cap with Jimmy's name on it over to Jesse, who already had the golf bag on his shoulder. He gave me a thumbs-up and stomped off to where the caddies and players were meeting while I went searching for Gabe.

⸙ ⸙ ⸙

We were at the first hole and Gabe was eating blue cotton candy he had gotten for free as we waited with the crowd to see Jimmy Savage off. There were cameras, kids, parents, and other celebrity golfers watching as Jimmy and Jesse stared at the clubs in Jimmy's bag. From the look on Jesse's face, I had the feeling that golf was not a sport he knew very much about. I didn't know much about it, either, but from the little I had seen on television, I knew that Jimmy was the first golfer ever to wear leather pants on the course.

I moved in closer to hear Jesse and Jimmy's conversation as Jimmy rummaged through the golf bag.

"Do I begin with the big ones and work down to the little ones?" he asked his caddy.

"Believe big and begin big," was the answer.

Jimmy pulled out a club with a big, wooden head on it.

"This?"

"Why not?" Jimmy answered.

The TV sportscaster was whispering into his microphone in that annoying way they do at golf tourneys. "Looks like Jimmy Savage is a novice, relying on the advice of his caddy. He's going to need some great coaching to beat Dweezil Zappa, who just birdied . . ." At that moment, Jimmy took a giant swing at the ball. The back swing nearly connected with his head. The crowd gasped at his close call, and the ball went sailing off into a water hazard, scattering ducks and landing on a muddy bank.

That was probably his best shot of the day. He went from water hazard to sand trap to water hazard until he was caked with mud. To his credit, his state of mind stayed positive. Maybe Jesse was feeding him "Willardisms" or maybe it was just his personality, but Jimmy seemed to be having a good time in spite of his pathetic showing.

The sportscaster continued whispering, "If Jimmy Savage keeps this up, he'll pull down the record of two hundred and sixty-three strokes for one game on this course."

The crowd was beginning to thin out a bit when Jimmy finally popped the ball out of his latest water hazard. Jesse executed a massive fist pump in triumph, and Jimmy smiled proudly.

"Now I know where I get my athletic ability," Gabe mumbled.

The sportscaster seemed to be so fed up that he wasn't even bothering to whisper anymore. He actually sounded pissed off. "Jimmy Savage would need an act of God to just stay in this competition, folks, and I don't think that's going to happen." He turned to the few fans that were left. "Let's move on to . . . anybody else in the game." And with that, he and the cameras moved off with most of the crowd.

Jimmy's next shot landed in a sand trap, and he and Jesse trudged after it with Gabe and me following. When we caught up, Jesse was on his knees brushing the sand away from the ball, trying to give Jimmy all the help he could. He handed him a club.

"So, kid," Jimmy said, "tell me something about yourself. Are you a fan of mine?"

"Yeah, I am."

"Can you tell me why?" Jimmy asked as he wound up and started his swing.

"'Cause you're my biological father," Jesse said. "I'm a 908 donor kid."

It was exactly at that moment that Jimmy connected. Scooping under the ball, he sent it flying straight up into the sun. He stood there, open-mouthed, staring at Jesse, oblivious to the fact that what goes up must come down. The ball bounced off Jimmy's head with a loud crack that made us all gasp. Then, with Jesse looking on in horror, Jimmy Savage dropped to his knees and fell face down into the sand.

chapter twenty-two

"Somebody call 911!" I screamed.

Gabe pulled my phone out of the back pocket of my jeans and held it up in front of my face.

"Why don't you?" he asked.

"Step one in an emergency is to say 'Call 911,'" I said, defending myself. "Now I will take step two, which is to actually do it." Inside I was kind of embarrassed as I punched in the numbers. "See, I'm doing this in logical order."

Jesse had turned Jimmy face up and was crouched next to him, listening to him breathe. Jimmy actually had a sweet, goofy smile on his face. The kind that people smile with their lips closed. He looked very happy and peaceful.

“He’s breathing okay,” Jesse told us, and Gabe and I both sighed with relief.

They must have had paramedics on the golf course, because two guys with a gurney appeared almost as soon as I turned off the phone. They got Jimmy into one of those things that stabilize your neck, lifted him onto the stretcher, and took off running toward the club entrance, where we could see the flashing lights of a waiting ambulance. We followed Jimmy and the EMTs, fighting our way through CVD kids and their parents.

The closer we got to the driveway, though, the harder it became for the paramedics to navigate the gurney. It seemed word had spread that Jimmy Savage had knocked himself out, and people were gathering from all over the golf course to take a look at him. He seemed to be even more interesting to them now that he was unconscious. The medic team kept yelling “Clear the way,” but everyone kept doing exactly the opposite, including the paparazzi, who were running alongside and snapping pictures of Jimmy.

We hit a bottleneck at the iron gates of the club entry, where another TV reporter was keeping the public up to date and loving every moment of the disaster. The dude was from one of those dumb shows that are all about celebrities, one of those shows that seem to be based on the idea that celebrities matter more than anyone else. You would have thought he was covering a state funeral from the serious tone of his voice.

“No good deed goes unpunished,” he philosophized. “Rock star and philanthropist, Jimmy Savage, has been struck down by his own ball during the first Celebrity CVD Golf Tournament. Perhaps his caddy can fill us in on the details."

The reporter grabbed Jesse's arm, stuck a mike under his nose, and asked one of those questions they all ask when something bad happens. "What is your name, son, and can you tell us what ran through your mind during that horrifying moment when Jimmy Savage was struck in the head, perhaps fatally, by his own golf ball?"

Jesse pushed the mike away with a "Get lost, dude."

The reporter took the hint and continued his show. "Jimmy Savage's caddy is too overcome with emotion to speak to us. We do not yet know the details of this accident, this golf swing gone terribly wrong, but our thoughts and prayers are with Jimmy."

It was then I realized that once they put Jimmy in the ambulance, we were going to lose him again. There was no way they'd believe we were his kids, no way they'd let us go with him. Then a plan occurred to me.

"Follow my lead," I whispered to Jesse and Gabe.

I grabbed a fistful of blue cotton candy and stuffed it into Gabe's mouth.

"Help!" I shrieked. "My brother is deathly allergic to blue food dye. He thought he was eating pink. He could die! Please help us."

Gabe clutched his throat and fell dramatically into Jesse's arms as the cameras swiveled to catch the latest drama. More EMTs rushed to his side as he uttered this amazing sound that combined choking and gagging. It sounded kind of like a combo of "Aaaaargh" and

"Gluuuugh," a phlegmy, gurgly scrape in his throat, and people standing near us looked as if they were going to puke. Little kids were crying in fear and clutching their parents. It was a beautiful thing, an Oscar-winning performance.

The TV guy was in *Access Insider Hollywood* heaven. His voice dropped an octave as Gabe was wheeled past him.

"Another tragedy, folks," the TV dude declared. "One of the most severely afflicted CVD kids ate the wrong color cotton candy and had a life-threatening allergic reaction, and now they are moving the young boy into the ambulance with Jimmy Savage. In seconds, the two of them, rock star and CVD kid, will be racing to the hospital together, perhaps racing for their lives."

I grabbed the arm of a nearby parking guard who was watching as they loaded Gabe. "We need to get our car out of the parking lot. That's our brother they're putting in the ambulance, and we have to follow him."

I looked up at him pitifully and choked out a sob.

Jesse put a protective arm around me. "They're very, very close," he said to the guard.

"Follow me," the guard told us. He yelled to the other guards, "Hey, help me get these kids out of here. Their brother's in the ambulance headed for the hospital. They're in 125, row C."

In an instant, the guards were throwing keys to each other, running around, and moving cars. Our guard took our ticket, pulled our keys off the parking board, and handed them to us with a tear in his eye. "I'll be praying for your brother," he said to me. "Stay hopeful."

"I guess I seriously better consider it," I told him. "You're the second person who's suggested that to me recently."

And with that, Jesse and I took off across the parking lot to the Jeep. A path had been opened ahead of us so we could zoom out of the lot and we did—just like members of the Lucky Sperm Club.

chapter twenty-three

When we got to the hospital, Gabe was in the emergency room, in an area marked TRIAGE. He spotted Jesse and me, slid off the gurney, and sneaked out the front door to meet us.

"Jimmy's on twelve, some kind of special VIP floor," he told us. "They told me you can't get up there without a pass." His eyes were gleaming; I could tell he was looking forward to the challenge of getting to our dad, and it was helping him bounce back from the Daisy heartbreak.

Who would have thought that a nerd would get so turned on by illegal escapades? I was finding out more and more that you really can't tell who people are just by looking at them.

We went inside and headed for the elevators in the main part of the hospital, but a guard stopped us. He wore lots of official looking badges, and his biceps looked like bowling balls.

"Fans wait out front," he ordered, checking out Jesse's Jimmy Savage cap.

"We're not fans," said Gabe. "I mean we are, but we're actually family."

"Yeah, yeah. Me too," said the guard. "But he wants privacy, so get lost."

"You're very tense," Jesse commented sadly. "Your chakras are definitely not in alignment."

"That's a shame, but I can live with it," snapped the guard. "Now get lost before I align my foot with your ass."

This was no place for "Willardisms." I took Jesse's arm, and the three of us retreated through the front door, where a laundry van had just pulled up into the driveway. The driver jumped out, opened the rear doors, and began unloading folded linen into a big canvas bin on wheels. Then he rolled the bin into the ER.

It took about twenty seconds for me to jump into the truck, grab some freshly laundered lab coats, and toss them to the guys. We hustled off just as the driver came back, slammed the doors closed, and slid back in behind the wheel.

We had just put on our doctor coats and were wondering what to do next when some nurses came out of a door marked STAFF ONLY next to the ER. It had no handle on the outside, just a key lock. I pulled Jesse's Jimmy Savage cap off his head, gave him a push in the right direction, and he raced over to grab the door before it closed. He flashed his golden boy smile at the nurses, who smiled back. When they'd gone, we dashed inside to find ourselves at the street-level entry to the hospital stairwell.

"Why did they have to put him on the top floor?" I asked as we started to climb.

"It's the floor for VIPs," Gabe told us. "The paramedic said it had special beds, a view of the ocean, and hot nurses. He said when Joan Rivers was here, she wanted to turn it into a time share."

The energy expended in climbing the stairs soon had Gabe wheezing and snorting.

"You don't sound so good," I told him. "Why don't you put one of those things on your nose?"

"I thought you hated the Breathe-Rite," he gasped.

"It's not that bad," I mumbled. "Just take it off before we meet Jimmy."

By the time we reached the seventh floor, I was huffing and puffing myself. Jesse didn't seem to be winded at all, but he suggested we take a rest and plunked himself down on one of the steps. I sat down on the same step, facing him, and Gabe settled down on the step just below us.

"We haven't had a chance to ask you, Swimmy," I said. "What went down with you and Willard?"

"I'll tell you," Jesse said warily, "but you have to promise not to laugh."

"We do," Gabe and I said in unison.

"Well," said Jesse, "I don't know if Willard is a nut, if he's really psychic, or if he's from another planet, but I do know he saw me in a way no one's ever seen me before."

"What do you mean?" asked Gabe.

"Seems like all my life I had this feeling that my insides and my outsides didn't match. I look like the dude who has everything. This . . ." He pulled at his face. "The jock thing, the popular thing. I tried to live in sync with that . . . like that was what mattered. But I always had this weird, empty feeling inside, even before Tina and Liz told me that they were splitting. Willard seemed to know all of that. He told me that it was okay. It was even a good thing for me to look inside myself for happiness instead of outside. He told me that I didn't have to worry about what anyone else did or what anyone else thought. I had to do what was right for me. He showed me how to relax and how to breathe, how to be in the moment and accept it, and how to feel my own presence. When I did what he told me, I felt a difference. He's the only person who ever understood that even though I had what everybody else wants, it only made me feel guilty instead of good."

"I love this. It's so anti-establishment," I said. "What else?"

"He gave me a list of books to read, gave me his phone number, and told me that I could call him any time to talk. Then he told me he believed I would find my path. All I had to do was look for it with an open heart."

"I'm sorta blown away," Gabe said, "even though it sounds like what my dad calls 'new age mumbo jumbo.'"

"Whatever it is," Jesse told him calmly, "I think there's something to it."

"You've changed since Willard," I told him. "In a good way."

"Thanks," said Jesse. "I don't usually let anyone know what I'm really feeling, but I had to tell both of you. It means a lot to me that you guys get it."

"I absolutely get it," I told him.

"Me too. And just for the record, I don't always agree with my dad," Gabe added.

"Let's go," I said, getting up. "At this moment, our path is vertical."

We trudged up the next five flights without talking, thinking about what Jesse had told us. It seemed like this trip was opening a lot of doors, but when we got to the twelfth floor, we found that a very important one wasn't going to open. The exit door from the stairwell to the hospital didn't have a handle.

"Someone's sure to use the stairs eventually," Jesse offered. "So let's just wait."

It was then that his phone started playing "Love Ya Moms" by Noreaga.

"Hi, Moms," he said in a phony, cheerful voice.

Why do we always use that voice when we're guilty about something?

"I'm good. I must have missed it 'cause I was in the shower. I sound echoey 'cause I'm at the pool. A couple of us are working out. We may enter some summer invitationals. Everything is cool.

Sorry, but its my turn to do laps. I gotta go now. Love you, too. Bye."

"How are they?" I asked.

"Maybe I haven't changed *that* much," Jesse laughed. "I forgot to ask."

Just then, we all came to attention. Someone was jiggling the handle on the hospital side of the door. We tried to look like we were having a consult about an upcoming surgery, but it didn't really matter. When the door finally opened, a gray-haired patient, an old guy in a hospital gown, backed in and slid a credit card against the lock as he closed it. Then he reached up and took a pack of cigarettes and a disposable lighter from the ledge over the door. He flicked the lighter a few times and cursed under his breath when nothing happened.

"You shouldn't smoke," Gabe said softly.

The dude almost jumped out of his slippers. He turned around to see who had spoken.

"Whaddaya know," he growled in a raspy voice. "Three Doogie Howsers."

"What's a Doogie Howser?" asked Gabe.

"Never mind," the old dude sighed. "You're too young to be alive."

"Smoking will shrink your chakra," Jesse warned him.

"If it shrinks my prostate, I'm outta here." He smiled. "Got a light?"

I pulled a book of matches I'd taken from the cantina out of my pocket and lit his cigarette. He inhaled to his toes as I shoved the matches into his hand, and the three of us exited the stairwell and replaced his card in the door.

"Try to cut down," I told him.

"If you say so, Doc," he called after us as the door closed on his Amex Platinum and we entered the exclusive world of ailing celebrities.

chapter twenty-four

It was a typical hospital floor layout, but everything was so much nicer. There was wallpaper on the walls and real hardwood floors. The nurses' station had vases filled with beautiful flowers. The doctors were all tall, dark, and handsome, straight out of Central Casting. The paramedic was right; the nurses looked more like model/actresses than medical assistants.

Most of the doors to the rooms were shut, so now that we were here, we had no idea how we were going to find Jimmy.

"What do we do now?" I asked Jesse as we went striding down the hall, trying to look as if we belonged. I think it was the first time I'd asked Jesse for advice, but he looked really good in that lab coat, almost like a real doctor on a TV show, and I was actually beginning to respect his opinion.

"I don't know yet, but the answer will find us," he answered. "Let's see what's gonna happen."

"What's gonna happen is that they're gonna throw us out of here," I told him.

"Hey, you guys," said Gabe. "Enemy at nine o'clock."

"This isn't a war movie," I grumbled. "Speak normally."

"Look over there at the nurses' station," he whispered.

Jesse and I looked over, and there, talking to a cute nurse, was our nemesis from the lobby, Mr. Bowling Ball Biceps, the hospital guard.

"Holy expletive deleted!" I gasped. "We gotta get out of here."

We were passing a door marked HOSPITAL EMPLOYEES ONLY, so we ducked in. It was a little lounge where the doctors and nurses probably sacked out or grabbed a cigarette during their time off. It reeked from tobacco, and there was a set of bunk beds with pillows and blankets.

"Grab a bed," Gabe ordered. "If anyone comes in, pull the blanket over your head. We gotta try to find a way to get Jimmy's room number, just in case the answer doesn't find us."

I turned out the light, and we each dove into a bed. I ended up with the bunk on top, but whatever.

"Maybe Jesse could call the hospital and say he's Jimmy's manager and he wants to know what room Jimmy's in," he went on.

"That won't work. He's probably got a code name or something, and we don't know it," I told him.

"We could wait until the middle of the night when there aren't as many nurses and peek in every room until we find . . ."

"Shhh," I whispered. I could hear the door opening.

"Hey, babycakes," a familiar voice crooned. "You got a fifteen-minute break and I'm a ten-minute man. We could definitely make this work."

It was the guard and one of the nurses. I heard the sound of someone being slammed up against the wall and then kissing and heavy breathing.

Oh my god! I thought. *They're going to do it here and now, right in this room, and we're going to have to listen.*

"Not now, honey bunch," Babycakes protested. "You never know who's gonna walk in."

"Or who's here," I wanted to shout.

"But that just makes it more fun, shorty," Biceps told her. There was more moaning and awful slurpy sounds.

Please don't let there be a reason for this to happen, I prayed.

Someone must have heard me, because just then the door opened.

"Hey, Rachel," said a female voice, "they want you in room 1212, stat."

"That's Jimmy Savage's room," the guard said. "Now don't you go falling in love."

Rachel giggled, and they both exited.

"You see," said Jesse, "the answer found us."

"If I remember correctly from when my mom had her appendix out," I told him, "the nurses usually change shifts at four. That means they're not in the patient's rooms, so I suggest we lay low for another hour and then head for Jimmy."

"Cool," Gabe commented. "Twelve-twelve isn't that far from here."

"We can do it," said Jesse. "Can you believe it? In an hour we'll be with our bio dad."

⁂

Promptly at four we walked out of the doctors' lounge and strolled down the hallway. The nurses' station was abuzz with the shift change. Gabe and I let Jesse walk ahead of us, counting on his smile to diffuse approaching trouble, but we didn't run into anyone. We opened the door to 1212 as silently as we could, slid inside, and closed it behind us.

It looked like a really nice hotel room. The hospital bed was huge and had a headboard and a dust ruffle. Jimmy was laying there with his eyes closed. He had an ice pack on top of his head, and it was impossible to tell if he was sleeping or still unconscious. He was snoring, though, a little like Gabe, but his snore had a cute little whistling echo.

We all leaned over the bed and looked at him intently.

"Damn if that's not my nose and chin," whispered Jesse. "Yours too, KT. And he's got a cowlick just like mine."

"And his hair's the exact color of ours," I added.

"And he's got a lot of it. I was worried about what that bandana was hiding," Jess said. "What a relief!"

Suddenly we heard the door handle turning. We looked at each other, totally panicked, and dove under the dust ruffle as if we were one person. I peeked out to see two sets of nurses' shoes entering.

"We're here to take your vitals, Mr. Savage," one of them said in that cheery nurse voice. "Your CT scan was clear, and you'll be feeling better in no time."

They bustled around, taking Jimmy's blood pressure and temperature and announcing the results. There wasn't a peep out of him.

"We'll be back later," the other one announced, and we heard the door close.

We slithered out from under the bed and gathered around Jimmy again. Suddenly he moaned a little. We all jumped. Then his eyelids started fluttering, and Jesse leaned over so that his face would be directly in Jimmy's line of vision. Jimmy's eyes opened. He stared blankly for a few seconds, and then we could see him beginning to remember. His wheels turned slowly, and then he stared at Jesse.

"You're the kid who said he's my son," he murmured weakly.

"I'm that kid," Jessie responded softly. "I got my files from Cryosperm, and my biological father was Donor 908."

"Then you really are my son," Jimmy whispered. "Wow!"

"Yes, sir, and I'm not alone," Jesse replied as Gabe moved in next to him.

"Me, too," Gabe asserted. "I'm your son, too."

A faint smile flickered over Jimmy's face. "Two sons," he whispered.

Then I moved into his view. "And you have a daughter, too," I told him.

Jimmy smiled even more broadly. "I love triplets. I'll be a great father, I promise. Don't do drugs, and don't call me sir."

And with that, he closed his eyes and either passed out or went back to sleep. The three of us hugged like crazy. We were all sniffling and pulling tissues out of the box on the nightstand. Then we stood there and watched Jimmy sleep for the longest time. When we heard someone coming, we crawled back under his bed to spend the night. I never knew sleeping on the floor could feel that good, but then again, I had never slept under my bio dad's bed before.

chapter twenty-five

The nurses kept coming in all through the night, checking on Jimmy and taking his vital signs. Then at six forty-five in the morning, his doctor showed up. I lifted the dust ruffle a smidge and saw an extremely cool pair of sandals topped with faded jeans standing next to the bed.

"Hey, Jim," a voice said gently, "how are you feeling?"

"I don't know, Doc," Jimmy said. "I'm sleeping."

I turned over on my back and looked up to see a doctor who looked just the way you'd want your doctor to look. He had thick white hair and a handsome, kindly face.

"Well, you're cleared to go home this afternoon, my man. No sports for the next week, and let me know if you have any dizziness, vomiting, or headaches. Anything weird, give me a call."

"I really want to go home, but something weird did happen last night, Doc," Jimmy whispered. "These teenagers were in my room, two boys and a girl, and they said they were my kids, which is crazy, and what's even crazier is that I knew they were telling the truth. They were wearing doctor coats, and no kid of mine would be old enough to be a doctor. Am I going nuts?"

"Sometimes people have very vivid dreams after a blow to the head," the doctor assured him. "It's nothing to worry about." And with that, the doc and his cool sandals turned and exited the room.

"Damn," said Jimmy out loud to himself. "It was so real."

We didn't know quite what to do. We didn't want to just jump out and scare him to death. So from under the bed I said, "You weren't dreaming. We're really here."

"You are?" Jimmy croaked, his voice a little shaky. "Where is 'here'?"

With that, we slithered out from under the bed and stood up. Jimmy's face lit up as if he had just won a Grammy.

"It wasn't a dream," he marveled. "You're my donor kids, and you're here. I'm so glad you're real, and you all must be geniuses. How else could you be doctors at your age?"

He patted the bed. "Get on board and give your old man a hug." We were more than happy to oblige.

Jimmy wanted to know all about us and how we found him. So we told him our individual stories and the story of our journey to track down our biological father. He listened intently to every word and asked really good questions. Every time a nurse or doctor would come in to see him, he'd introduce us proudly, and everyone would look at us like we were really special. He even had them run a blood typing on him so we could see he was Type A. I insisted they do a DNA test, as well, so he would know we were his kids, although with Jess and me, you just had to look at us. Jimmy was all for it and told them to "put it on his tab."

"I hope you'll come home with me," Jimmy said. "Spend at least a few days with your dad."

"We'd really like to do that," Gabe said.

"More than anything in the world," I added.

"I love the beach," Jesse chimed in.

"How'd you know I live in Malibu?" Jimmy asked. "You read *Rolling Stone?*"

"No," I said, "he just knows things."

"Cool," said Jimmy, and that was that.

While Jimmy was getting dressed, Jesse and I called our moms. I told my mom that I would be staying at Sasha's for a few extra days, that her folks were cool with it, and not to worry. It sounded as if she was busy with Ben and work, so it was easy to pull off, but I had to put a lot of effort into being my usual snarky self because I felt so incredibly happy. I didn't want to sound too different and set off a maternal alarm.

Jesse carried on to his moms about how delicious the dinners that they had left him were, and how he was having a great time laying low at home. He made up some good stuff about calling the plumber so everything wouldn't sound too perfect.

When Jimmy came out of the bathroom, all dressed and ready to go, he gave our car keys to someone who brought the Jeep around to a secret celebrity exit so we could avoid the paparazzi who were waiting out front.

Jimmy took one look at the jumble of luggage in the Jeep and immediately rearranged all of it so that there was more room. "It's my roadie experience," he explained.

Jesse took the wheel, and we all piled in. It was kind of amazing to me that Jimmy didn't mind riding in our old wreck. He seemed to get a kick out of it, and we talked and sang and carried on like the happy, nutty family I never thought I would have. That ecstatic mood lasted for the whole ride.

After about an hour, we got to this place called The Colony on Malibu Beach. We passed a guardhouse, and the guards looked shocked that a junk heap like ours would be trying to get in. But when Jimmy gave them a smile and a wave, they let us roll right through.

Jimmy's house didn't look like much from the outside, but when you walked into it, it was like walking into another world. One whole wall of the living room was made of sliding glass doors that opened onto a deck jutting out over the beach. Surfers were riding waves, people were running along the water line, others were throwing sticks for their dogs, and kids were building sand castles. It was like paradise.

The house was super modern and open, and the huge living room was filled with big boy toys. There were pinball and popcorn machines, video games, a pool table, a gigantic flat screen TV on a wall surrounded by six other smaller screens, and every high-tech gadget known to man. You could even open the glass doors just by pushing a button.

The kitchen was separated from the living room by a wide counter with comfy stools in front of it, and every available surface was filled with bowls of fruit, jars of candy, and plates of cookies. There was a restaurant style stove and a refrigerator the size of our apartment back in St. Louis. The three of us must have looked the way Dorothy did when she found herself in the Land of Oz.

As we stood there, a good-looking, twenty-something guy with a BlackBerry in his hand came racing toward us and began babbling to Jimmy.

"Thank god you're here! Your manager called, your agent called, your publicist called, your record company called, your nutritionist emailed, your masseuse left a message, everyone—" Jimmy held up his hand, signaling "Hold it."

"This is Alex, my assistant," he told us. "Alex, this is my daughter, KT, and my sons, Jesse and Gabe. I was a sperm donor back in the day, and these are my kids."

Alex's mouth fell open. Jimmy went on. "Cancel everything until my concert, except rehearsals. I'm spending quality time with my children." He put his arms around our shoulders. "Your daddy's gonna make it all up to you."

We just stood there grinning like idiots when suddenly a voice yelled, "Jimmykins!" and a redheaded model-actress type, in the shortest cutoff jeans I've ever seen, came running into the room and threw her arms around Jimmy.

Jimmy unwrapped her arms. "Hey, baby," he said, "I want you to meet my kids from when I was a sperm donor. This is KT and Jesse and Gabe. Kids, this is Brandy. She does my makeup, among other things."

"I do him, too," Brandy informed us. "Don't I, baby?"

"Hey, Bran, cool it. These are my kids," said Jimmy. He playfully put his hands over my ears and turned to Brandy. "So listen, darlin', you know I'm seriously nuts about you, but you're gonna have to excuse me for the next little while, 'cause these three are gonna be my priority."

"Of course they are," Brandy agreed. "They should be." Still, she didn't look very happy about it.

Jimmy gave her a cute, loud smooch on the cheek. "She's the one, my children. After a lot of years of looking, I finally found true love."

"You are the sweetest," Brandy gushed.

"Have Maria fix us some lunch, Bran, and then . . ." Jimmy paused and then announced dramatically, "let the spoiling begin."

For some reason I still don't understand, we all jumped up and down and clapped our hands like preschoolers. We could tell that Jimmy thought that was adorable, but Brandy? Well, not so much.

chapter twenty-six

When we came out after lunch, the Jeep had been completely unloaded.

"Your stuff's in the guesthouse," Jimmy told us.

"You sure you want to drive this heap?" I asked him.

"Yeah," he said, "it's perfect. The paps would never guess I'd be driving something like this. We're undercover for real. Today is gonna be all for you, my children, and don't ask me where we're going. It's going to be a surprise."

"Hang for just a second," Gabe said. "I gotta go back for my nasal spray."

"Don't forget your Breathe-Rites," I called after him. When Gabe came back out, Jimmy jumped behind the wheel. We piled in and hit the road.

Our first stop was this place called Griffith Park. Jimmy scooted through the park, head down so no one would recognize him, and we trailed after him like he was the Pied Piper.

"There's a great observatory here," Gabe told me. "Maybe that's where we're going." But it wasn't.

We pulled up in front of an old-fashioned merry-go-round, the kind with big painted horses from the olden days. A huge organ was piping out songs from *Mary Poppins*. We didn't know what to say, so we didn't say anything.

Jimmy was positively glowing. "I always wanted to have a reason to go on this," he crowed.

None of us wanted to rain on his parade, so we each climbed on a horse, as did he. We rode around for what seemed like forever, 'round and 'round and up and down, and on and on and on. When it finally stopped, Jimmy jumped off and went dashing across the park again with us in tow. We had to run to keep up with him. We had no chance to talk to each other, but we communicated with various levels of eye rolling. We understood each other so well that words weren't necessary.

The next stop was the pony rides. Thankfully, Jimmy let us ride the faster ponies for age seven and over, but even so, the stirrups were so short that Jesse's knees were up around his shoulders. Jimmy stood behind the fence with the other parents and glowed with pride as we trotted by. He was the only one who didn't notice that everyone was laughing at us.

After that it was the zoo. Not the real zoo, which might

have been fun (even though I don't approve of zoos unless it's the new kind where the animals have natural habitats). We were taken to the petting zoo, where we were surrounded by goats, sheep, and pigs. It was like Willard's, but not as nice. Jimmy even paid extra so that we could get brushes to brush the animals.

"What do you think is going on in his head?" I asked Gabe as we crouched near each other, brushing the goats.

"I think Jimmy is making up for the years he missed by starting at the beginning," Gabe whispered. His nose was beginning to stuff up, but he was hanging in there.

"Can we say something?" I asked.

"Look at him," Gabe said. "What do you think?"

I looked over at Jimmy. He was happily brushing a sheep next to Jesse, who wore a sweet, contented look on his face. Our dad was smiling and singing to the sheep, and Jesse was saying to him: "You really should consider not eating anything with a face. It will enhance your aura and ratchet up your energy."

"I get your message, my boy child," Jimmy replied solemnly.

After an hour there, Jimmy gathered us together. "Our next stop is just for my little girl," he told us, grinning at me tenderly. "You're gonna love it."

"I can't wait," I told him. What else could I say? He looked so damn sweet.

We drove to a shopping mall called The Grove, and Jimmy gave Jesse and Gabe money for snacks and told them to wait for us while he and I went inside the American Girl Shop. I couldn't believe that place. I guess I would have loved it when I was eight, but now it looked to me like a training ground for preteen terrorist consumerism. There were dolls of all ethnicities, and you could even have a doll made to look like you. Jimmy insisted that we have that done. There were doll books, doll accessories, doll hair salons, and a photo shop where you could have a picture taken with your doll (Jimmy insisted on that one, too). We walked out to meet Gabe and Jesse, loaded with more dolls than we could carry. Jimmy was beaming proudly and showing off the photo of me with my look-alike doll.

Next, we stopped off at Chuck E. Cheese, but we didn't eat. We just slid down the tube slides and jumped unhappily in a ball pit with some preschoolers. Then we caught a break. One of the moms there recognized Jimmy, and a pack of them began to mob him for autographs. He gave us a signal, and we got out as fast as we could.

When we got home, Maria had cooked up regular and vegetarian hamburgers and hot dogs and set up a picnic in the living room in front of the big-screen TV. At last, I thought, maybe some juvenile but grownup entertainment on the tube, but it was not to be. Jimmy had sent Alex to the video store, and what popped up on the screen? A Wiggles DVD.

Jimmy leaned back and sighed. "This was the best day of my life," he said. "I love being a dad."

We all looked at each other. Could we say it?

"It was great, so great, beyond great . . . it was truly magnificent," I said.

Gabe picked up with, "It was, and Jimmy, please don't think we don't appreciate everything you've done. I mean the merry-go-round reminded me of when I was a lot younger, and I used to love to do that kind of stuff . . ."

"But, Jimmy, the truth is, although the petting zoo was very cool, we're not actually little kids anymore," Jesse said very gently. "That ship has kind of sailed."

Jimmy's face fell for an instant. He looked at us with so much affection, it made me choke up. Then he hit himself in the forehead. "What was I thinking?" he asked the universe. "Of course, you need more grown-up entertainment. Tomorrow will be different." That taken care of, he moved on.

"Now let me show you how this TV set-up works. Each one of the smaller screens is hooked up to another place in the house, so I can be sitting here and see what's happening in the recording studio, the control room, the pool, the spa, the front door, and the deck. You just press the button with the letter of the area you want to see. If you press it twice, you can tape what's going on there. Press the button three times, and the action pops up on the big screen. Cool, huh?"

"The coolest," we told him.

"So if you need me, you can just look for me."

"Finding you in this house is a snap," I told him, "compared to just plain finding you."

"What should we do now?" Jimmy asked. "Wanna watch one of my concerts?"

That's what we all wanted, so that's what we did next. Now it was our turn to feel proud. Our dad may have had a reputation as a wild man, but he was such a bitchin' singer and songwriter, I felt blessed to have inherited even a hangnail of his talent. About midnight we all said goodnight, and the three of us headed back to the guesthouse. Gabe and Jesse were sharing a room and I had one to myself, at least I thought so until I opened the door.

Sitting on my bed, wearing a lacy, baby-doll night thing and doing her nails, was Brandy. What was with all these manicures around me suddenly?

"Hi, KT," she said. "I hope you don't mind that I let myself in."

What could I say? That I did mind?

"That's okay, Brandy," I said. "What's up?"

"I just wanted to chat with you a bit. You know, a little girl talk," she explained.

"Lay it on me." I plopped down on the bed facing her.

"Well, Jimmy and I are very close, as you may have guessed."

"Couldn't miss it," I assured her.

"I may be a little overprotective of him, but that's how I am. I'd never let anyone come between us."

"Chill out, Bran," I told her. "There's no way we can do for him what you do."

She leaned forward. "Not that it's any of my business, but exactly how long are you and your brothers planning to be here?"

"You said it, that's between us and our . . . Jimmy."

"I could try to get all BFFy with you and your brothers, especially the cute one, but I'm too up front for that, so I'll just say it. I don't know who you really are or why you really came here. I kind of figure it's 'cause he's a rich rock star. His brain may be a little fried from his druggie years, but I want you to know that I'm here to protect him, to keep his focus on making music and keeping his bank account full. That's what matters. He doesn't need the distraction of the three of you. So what it comes down to is, the sooner you leave, the sooner he can get back to what he's supposed to be doing—his music and me."

She sighed and stood up. "And don't think you can mess with me, KT," she said. "I'd hate to have to screw up your relationship with your . . . Jimmy. But I could do it like that." She snapped her fingers. "Damn, I smudged a nail," she fussed. *Could be karma,* I thought, but I didn't say it. Then she picked up her nail polish and sashayed out the door.

I sat there wondering how she could screw up our relationship with Jimmy when there was a knock on my door. It was Gabe and Jesse, and I filled them in on my visitor.

"That's really interesting," said Gabe. "I've been waiting until we were alone, without Jimmy, to tell you guys, but today when I ran back in the house for my allergy spray, I spied Miss Brandy and Alex engaged in some serious tongue wrestling. It was very uncool. Jimmy really loves her, and I think she's just with him for the rock star perks."

"Maybe things do happen for a reason," Jesse mused. "Maybe we were sent here to save our dad."

"We can't tell him about any of this. She'll just deny it," I said.

"We can't tell him, but maybe we can show him. I heard them talking about hooking up while we're out tomorrow," Gabe told us.

"Let's beat this one out," I said. "It should be a lot easier than getting through Texas, and we managed to do that."

So we put our heads together again, and before we knew it, the "Savages" had a plan for Operation Save Our Dad.

chapter twenty-seven

The next morning we came into the house to find Jimmy and Brandy sucking face and having breakfast at the kitchen counter. When he saw us, Jimmy got all flustered like we had seen something we shouldn't have. He gave Brandy a gentle nudge to push her away, as if to say "not in front of the kids."

"Mornin', my children," he said, his attention totally transferred to us. "Let me lay out today's game plan. Tomorrow night's the concert, so this morning the band's coming over to run down a few songs in the studio. I thought you might like to sit in on that."

Might like to? We were totally pumped.

"And this afternoon," Jimmy went on, "I've arranged something special to make up for yesterday's mistakes." He turned to Brandy. "Hey, sweet thing, why don't you go shopping or something while I hang with my babies?"

He pressed some cash into her hand, and Brandy's face was a picture of mixed emotions. "Money" and "shopping" equaled "good" and "happy," but "Jimmy and us alone" equaled "bad" and "sad." She took the money and disappeared, but I could feel her resentment hanging in the air.

We munched out until the band arrived. There was Toxic, the bass player, a beanpole of a dude totally covered in tattoos. Louie "Fingers" Lemonchello was on synth and keyboards. He was chubby and balding, and both he and Toxic had been in Jimmy's old band, Bad Angels. Then there was the drummer, "Sticks" O'Conner, and "Big Dee" Willis, who played guitar, any other instrument needed, and sang vocal parts with Jimmy.

Jimmy clicked on the camera in the studio, and we could see Alex in there setting up for rehearsal. "We're coming in, my man," Jimmy told him. For the next two hours, I was in heaven listening to my bio dad's music and watching how he worked with his musicians. He may have been a nut in his private life, and he may have forfeited some gray matter to his excesses, but he was still a pro in the studio.

Then it came time for our grown-up afternoon entertainment. Jimmy was waiting in his car for us. Gabe, of course, had to run back in for his spray, but we took off all excited.

"Hey, Jimmy," Gabe said, "I think the camera in the studio isn't working."

"I'll check it when we get back," Jimmy told him.

I guess we should have known that Jimmy didn't have a clue as to what kids our age considered fun, but it didn't really hit home until we drove through a neighborhood of mansions called Holmby Hills. Jimmy turned into a gated driveway and proceeded to a huge semicircular parking area around a big fountain. He just sat there grinning until the doors opened, and an old dude in pajamas and a bathrobe came out to the car.

"I'm Hugh Hefner. You can call me Hef," the dude said. "Welcome to the Playboy Mansion. Jimmy tells me you're in need of adult entertainment."

Oh my god! Wrong, so wrong, on so many levels. I mean, I actually wrote an extra credit paper in social studies, "The Birth of Feminism." I once had a goldfish I named Steinem, after Gloria. Everything in me wanted to scream "Get me out of here! This is a disgusting place where women are exploited." But I just couldn't do it. First of all, I wasn't sure Jimmy would even understand the whole concept without a long explanation that would hurt his feelings. And second, he was grinning proudly because he was delivering his big special surprise.

Our dad was trying so hard to make us happy in his own sweet, misguided way, it just seemed kinder to roll with it. For some reason, I was beginning to understand a lot more about being kind.

Hef took us to the game house, which had even more toys, video games, and jukeboxes than Jimmy's house. There were beautiful "bunnies" wandering around who all seemed to be named Kendra, Brittany, or Chloe. And a lot of people looked kind of familiar, like they might be celebrities. In no time, Jimmy was surrounded by hot chicks and fans, and as they dragged him away, he held up his cell phone and called out to us, "I'll be at the Grotto. Call me if you need me. Have fun." I guess he forgot that he had never given us his cell phone number. When Hef finally left us on our own, the three of us settled down on a couch.

"Jimmy is such a great guy," Jesse said solemnly.

"The greatest," Gabe added.

"The best ever," I chimed in.

"He's got the biggest heart," Gabe continued.

"And he's a lot of fun," Jesse commented.

"We're so lucky," I said.

"We are," Gabe declared. "We're the Lucky Sperm Club."

We sat there in silence, lost in our own thoughts. Finally, I got up the guts to say it: "You know, he's not exactly the dad I thought we were gonna find."

"I know what you mean," Gabe said.

"He has a very young soul," Jesse remarked.

"Yeah," I went on, "he's like a vacation. It's great for a while but not, like, forever. You know, basically he's like an old kid."

"Yeah, I'm kind of over the healthy junk food," Gabe added. "He's not really the dad my moms are," Jesse mused. "I don't think it's in his DNA."

Just then, a Playboy bunny in a bikini danced up to us. "Jimmy sent me," she announced. "We're gonna play water volleyball, and we'd like you to join us."

"I don't think so," Gabe and I both answered.

"I hate to be rude when a path is being revealed, but I didn't bring my bathing suit," said Jesse.

"Don't worry," the bunny assured him. "I'll take mine off." And with that she whisked him away.

I pulled out my phone. "You're so lucky your parents are out at sea, and you don't have to check in," I told Gabe.

"I guess so," he sighed, "but I kind of miss them."

"Hi, Mom," I said, "I didn't think I'd get you home. I miss you, too, but we're getting some real good work done."

My mom said I was sounding happier than usual. "I sound happier 'cause I am," I told her. "I know it's unusual. I'm happy that you're happy that I'm happy. Have fun with Ben. Sasha says hi. I love you. Bye."

"That's that," I said to Gabe.

"What do we do now?" he asked.

"We could play video games until J and J turn up," I told him. So that's what we did. Gabe killed me, but I didn't mind.

We didn't say anything to Jimmy about what a bad choice the Playboy Mansion was for us. He and Jesse had fun playing volleyball so we acted as if it had been a perfect afternoon.

When we got back to Malibu, Jimmy headed straight for the TV remote. He hadn't forgotten what Gabe had told him.

"Let's see what's wrong with this thing," he announced and clicked S for Studio. "Let's see if it taped rehearsal." He punched the button three times.

First the time, 3:00 p.m., came up on the big, dark screen. The rehearsal had ended at two. Then an image popped on. There were Brandy and Alex, but they weren't rehearsing. They were making out like crazy, giving a full-out performance, with vocals, on the studio floor. Jimmy clicked it off right away and turned to us with a really hurt look in his eyes.

"This is a life lesson that I never want you to have to learn, my children," he said sadly. "Over the years, I've found that the easiest relationship for me is with ten thousand people, and the hardest is with one."

"Not if it's the right one," I told him.

The wounded look on his face made me feel really bad.

"Don't close your heart," Jesse advised. "Just keep your eyes open."

"You deserve the best, and she wasn't it," said Gabe.

"You guys are very smart. I'm glad you're here," Jimmy said sincerely. "Now I have some business to take care of. I'll see you later."

With that he walked out of the room and we headed back to the guesthouse. We'd saved him, but we'd hurt him, too. Nothing ever seemed to be as clear-cut as I used to think it was.

"He'll be okay," Jesse told us. "The right someone is waiting to come into his life. It's just a matter of time."

chapter twenty-eight

When we came back to the house at dinnertime, Brandy and Alex were gone. We never saw them again, not that we wanted to. Jimmy was a little quiet and didn't mention what had gone down. We had dinner out on the deck, and afterward, Jesse and Gabe left to take a walk on the beach.

Jimmy had just gone to get his guitar from the studio when my phone began playing "Hungry Heart" by The Boss. I got really scared because that was my mom's ringtone and I had already talked to her. When I picked up, she was crying, and I found out why between sobs. Hearts were being broken right and left today.

"Please, Mom, don't cry," I pleaded. "How could you know Ben was on parole? My god, he was on JDate."

I listened as she beat herself up, and then I cut in.

"Mom, I know you can't see it now, but this is for the best. He wasn't the one. I know how bummed you must be, I can feel it through the phone, but please try and believe that everything happens for a reason. Don't be so hard on yourself. Just let it go. I love you too, Mom," I told her. "I'll be home soon, and you'll feel better after we eat some Ben and Jerry's and watch *Sleepless in Seattle.*"

I clicked off, picked up my guitar, and began noodling like I always do when I'm upset. Jimmy must have heard some of my conversation with Mom, because after he moseyed in, his first question was, "Do you want to tell me about it?"

I kept on playing. "It's my mom. Someone let her down and she's not doing so well."

"I can relate," he said. "What's Mom like?"

"She's sweet, and she's pretty, and she's lonely," I told him. "All she does is hook up with losers, probably on account of me.

"What do you mean?" Jimmy asked.

"She thinks I need a dad."

"Do you?"

"I thought so, but now I don't know. Now that I think about it, maybe all I wanted was to find out who he was. Finding you was really all that I needed."

He picked up his own guitar and began weaving in and out of my picking.

"So now that you found me, what do you think?" he asked.

"I think I'm okay, sorta happy actually," I said, and I couldn't help but smile at the way our playing fit together. It was like dancing with the perfect partner.

"I love your smile, my girl child," Jimmy said. "I used to think I couldn't be a good writer if I was happy, but over the years I found out that even though pain can make the creative juices flow, sometimes happiness can make them positively percolate."

"I'm beginning to get that," I told him. "Hey, you gonna play this one tomorrow night?" I asked and then segued into the opening riff of one of my favorite Bad Angel songs, "Undefeated."

Jimmy smiled and joined me, and then we started to sing together. Our blend was awesome. It was as if we'd harmonized forever. When the song ended, we heard applause and looked up to see that Jesse and Gabe had come back from their walk.

"That was incredibly cool," Gabe said.

"You can't imagine what it felt like for me," Jimmy said.

"Thanks for the gift," I whispered.

"You're welcome, baby girl," Jimmy said. "It's the least I could do."

The room was so loaded with emotion, we had to get out of there. "Hey," Jimmy said, "let's roast some marshmallows on the beach."

Jesse got a fire going and we all sat around it. The night was cool, the fire was blazing gold and orange, and silver streaks of moonlight bounced off the waves as they rolled in to shore. We all sat there silently, taking in the sounds of the beach and the warmth of the starry California night. Then Jess cleared his throat, kicked off his hemp sandals, and dug his toes into the sand.

"I've made up my mind where I'm gonna live," he said, breaking the silence.

"I'd be really honored and happy to have you hang with me if it's okay with your moms," Jimmy told him.

"Thanks, Jimmy, but Tina's giving up her home and her business. I think she's gonna need me. No, I *know* she's gonna need me. I hate moving, changing schools and all that, but I love my mom, so that's what I have to do."

"How'd you figure that one out?" Jimmy asked.

"I just listened to my heart," Jesse explained.

We all took that in while Jimmy handed out sticks with marshmallows on them. Then Gabe blew his nose and asked the big question he'd been waiting to ask for so long.

"Jimmy, when you were my age, were you allergic to anything?"

"Nope," Jimmy said.

Gabe's face fell.

"I was allergic to *everything,*" Jimmy continued. "I sneezed and snorted all the time. I almost forgot about that."

"How did you get over it?"

"I grew up, Gabe. Well, not really, but I guess I grew out of it."

"Then there's hope for me," Gabe said, grinning.

"Don't even doubt it, my man," Jimmy said, giving

him an encouraging pat on the shoulder. "One day you'll wake up and it'll be a little better. Then one day, like magic, it'll be gone."

"Like magic. I like that," Gabe breathed. "When my dad used to tell me that, I didn't believe it because he always puts a positive spin on stuff."

"That sounds like a good thing," Jimmy commented.

"Yeah, my dad's a really, really good guy."

"Tell me about him."

"Well, when I was five, he got me my own little Butcherelli Auto Shop uniform and told me that he hoped I would follow in his footsteps. Then when I was nine and won first prize at a science fair, he sat me down and said, "I think my footsteps may be too small for you."

"That's heavy and kind of wonderful," Jimmy said. "You're lucky to have a dad like that."

"What was your childhood like?" I asked Jimmy.

"Not good," he sighed, licking a marshmallow from his fingers. "My dad died when I was two and my mom remarried. He was a bad guy. He drank a lot, and he beat me up a lot. I took off as soon as I graduated from high school and never looked back. I wanted to start all over. I even changed my name."

"What was your real name?" I asked.

"Savitsky," said Jimmy. "Jacob Savitsky."

"But your tattoos, the cemetery thing."

"I know, I know. That's what my mom said, but what better way is there for a nice Jewish boy to rebel? Now that I've rehabbed and Twelve-Stepped, I'm not as pissed off anymore, and sometimes I wish I could erase my tats . . . except for Donor 908 'cause that's how you guys found me."

"So we're all half-Jewish. I can't wait to tell my BFF, Sasha. I skipped getting a tat because of her. Now I guess I could only ink half of me. If you were me, would you do it? I'm a rebel just like you."

"It's up to you, my girl child. Listen to your heart. Hey . . ." Jimmy's face suddenly brightened with an impish grin. The conversation was getting too heavy for him, I could tell.

"How about we tell ghost stories now?" he suggested.

We stayed on the beach until way past midnight. It was amazing how much fun it was just telling stories and trying to scare each other, acting silly and laughing . . . just being together. It was something I'd never even dared to dream about. It was heaven until we had to remind Jimmy that he had a concert the next night and he better get some sleep. Then we all walked up to the house with our arms around each other's shoulders, and my brothers and I tucked our dad into bed and turned out his light.

chapter twenty-nine

I came into the house the next morning to find Gabe gazing down at the beach while he ate his breakfast on the deck.

"What's so interesting down there?" I asked as I poured some orange juice.

"Take a look," he responded.

I looked down to see Jimmy and Jesse walking a labyrinth made out of sand.

"When did Swimmy build that?"

"Early this morning," Gabe told me. "When Jimmy came in, he started asking Jesse about his hemp sandals, and Jess asked him if he'd like to walk the labyrinth with him. That was an hour and a half ago."

"Something tells me that Jimmy's path is going to be revealed," I said. "You know, we're a very weird family."

"But we're a family," Gabe said.

"I guess we are. And we each have two: our families back home and the one we've made for ourselves . . . with Jimmy. Maybe *that's* why we're the Lucky Sperm Club."

Just then, a surfer in a wet suit and facemask walked past Jimmy and Jess. They all nodded at each other the way people do when they pass on the beach.

"There's something familiar about that dude in the wet suit. It's the way he walks or something," I told Gabe.

"You probably just saw him yesterday."

"I guess so," I said, as Jimmy and Jesse spotted me and headed back up the stairs to the house.

⸙ ⸙ ⸙

That evening, we piled into a limo with Jimmy and rode down to The Forum. It was only six, and the concert didn't begin until eight. But fans were already gathering.

Jimmy looked down at Jesse's hemp sandals. "Those shoes really do speak to me," he said. "They're more than shoes."

Jesse smiled. "Yeah, they are."

"Hemp and I were very close until rehab," Jimmy continued. "But now I'm looking at the weed in a whole new way." He threw Jesse a look. "I'm looking at a lot of things in a new way."

It was then that the fans somehow figured out that Jimmy was in the limo. Someone screamed his name, and the crowd began rushing toward us. Seeing what was happening, the driver sped up and turned into a secure, chain-link protected, VIP area. At the same time, security moved in to control the sea of shrieking Jimmy fanatics.

"It's a little scary being a rock star," I said to Jimmy.

"Not half as scary as being a dad," he told me.

We got out of the car and walked through the tunnel to backstage. Jimmy's new assistant, Chris, met us and draped backstage passes around our necks.

"What's up, my brother?" Jimmy asked him.

"Nobody's outrageously drunk or noticeably high," Chris reported.

"These are my babies, man: KT, Jesse, and Gabe. Keep an eye on them."

"Will do," Chris assured him. "Sound check was cool. Big Dee sang for you."

"That taken care of, it's time to rock and roll."

Jimmy moved into work mode now. He was speeding down the dimly lit hall so fast that the rest of us had to jog to keep up with him.

"Listen up, my children, while I run down the rules."

"We've been to concerts before," I told him.

"Not with me, so pay attention. Do not go to the bathroom. Do not drink anything that doesn't have a sealed cap. Do not eat anything but Fritos, Cheetos, and fruit."

"I'm good with fruit," Jesse let him know.

We turned down another hall and there was Toxic, the bass player. A hot blonde was all over him.

"Hey, Tox. Looking lovely, Desiree," said Jimmy.

They gave us all a little wave, and Desiree winked at Gabe. Jimmy didn't slow up, and Chris jumped in front of him to open the door to the dressing room. A heavyset, forty-something woman with piercings was waiting inside. She was Jimmy's new makeup lady, and she had all his stuff laid out.

"You guys know Toxic from rehearsal, but you don't *know* Toxic," Jimmy went on. "Just let me just say that I would prefer you did not get too close to him. I saw the wink, Gabe, and Desiree is not a nice girl. She's not monogamous, if you know what I mean. She thinks they have an open relationship, and Toxic doesn't. It makes him crazy. I mean vicious crazy, looking-for-a-fight, busting-someone's-head-crazy. So beware, Gabe. The rest of the band is benign, although be sure to decline anything in the way of smokes that Fingers may offer you. And if Sticks wants to help you clear your nose, Gabe, just say no politely. Do not stand too close to the speakers, stay out of the roadie's way, pick up your feet so you don't trip on wires and unplug anything, and watch your step in general."

"Is there anything we *can* do?" I asked.

"Listen to your dad."

He tossed Jesse a pair of sneakers.

"Can I borrow those grass slippers, Jess?"

"Sure." Jesse flipped off his sandals, put on the sneakers, and grinned. "Same big feet."

"Now why don't you guys hang outside for a while?"

We all started to leave, but Jimmy had something on his mind. "Hey, Gabe, stick around a minute."

Jess and I went out, waited a second, looked at each other, and glued our ears to the door. Something was up and we didn't want to miss out on it.

"What's with you, kid?" Jimmy was asking Gabe. "This concert scene not your thing?"

"I'm good," said Gabe.

"Hey Shiloh," Jimmy said softly to the makeup lady, "give us five, okay?"

Jesse and I jumped away from the door as the makeup lady exited. Fortunately, she headed down the hall toward the food spread instead of staying with us. We leaned our heads against the door again.

"Tell me," Jimmy said.

There was a moment of silence. Whatever it was, it wasn't easy for Gabe to talk about. Finally, the words came.

"It's like this," he said. "I see your talent in KT, but I'm so tone-deaf, I flunked chorus. You and Jesse have a million things in common. You're both . . ."

"Really good looking. Here, Gabe, put my boots in the closet." "Yeah, you are," said Gabe.

"Catch my socks," Jimmy directed.

"Maybe we should have another DNA test or something. KT and Jess look just like you, but there doesn't seem to be any of you in me."

Jimmy's voice was intense. We could almost see him leaning forward and looking Gabe in the eyes. "Listen to me, Gabe," he said. "I have to work really hard at liking myself. You come to it naturally. I have to work really hard at being the kind of person I want to be. You do it as easy as pie.

You're the unscrewed-up me I might have been if Joe Butcherelli had been my dad. We're connected on a very deep level."

You could tell he meant it.

"Hey," said Gabe. "Check out your toes . . ."

"What do you mean?"

"And check out mine."

Jimmy let out a belly laugh. "You got it. You got the Savitsky webbed toe."

"The Savitsky toe," Gabe marveled. "That's something special."

"So are you, my boy child," said Jimmy. "And now you've got something of me to pass on to your kids."

They both laughed. Jesse and I peeked in. They were doing some hug-substitute punching that ended up in the real thing. We closed the door silently.

"Don't . . ."

"Talk to Desiree. I know."

And Gabe walked out to join us.

"Guess what," he said. We let him tell us what had happened because it was a way for him to relive the moment, and we didn't want him to know how nosy we were. He looked as if he had just won the lottery.

We could hear the excitement building out front. The crowd was beginning to clap impatiently when Chris came up to us. "Clear the hall and come with me. It's showtime."

chapter thirty

Then Jimmy, followed by the band, moved quickly through the wings toward the stage. We stood aside and kept our heads down so as not to look at Desiree.

"My lady," Jimmy said, seemingly to no one, and a roadie placed a guitar in his outstretched hand. He stopped in front of us as the band dashed on stage and manned their instruments. The audience grew even more excited and began chanting, "Jim-my. Jim-my. Jim-my."

"I want you to stay right here where I can see you," he told us. "You okay, KT?" I nodded. "This show is dedicated to all of you." And with that, Jimmy Savage took the stage.

The power of his voice and guitar and the band's energy on the opening song, "Undefeated," blasted the audience out of their seats and to their feet. His performance made them believe that they could do anything, that they, too, could be undefeated. It was amazing to look at their faces and see how his music could transform them and make them invincible for that moment.

The three of us looked out on a sea of fist-pumping, screaming rock and rollers. Some were in their twenties and others were in their thirties and even forties. Some had come with their kids, and all of them were taking off on the rocket ship that was Jimmy Savage.

They were loving Jimmy, and they were filling him up with that love, making him forget all the bad things that had ever happened to him. It was such an intense love affair, I understood why Jimmy felt that having a relationship with ten thousand people was easier than having a relationship with one person. The song ended to cheers and applause and cries of "We love you, Jimmy." He let them carry on for a while, and then he held up his hands for quiet.

"Thank you, everybody," he said. "I want to share something with you tonight." He paused to milk it. "I just became a father."

The audience went nuts, whistling and applauding.

"Seems about seventeen years ago, I was a sperm donor and my biological kids just found me. Fortunately, I wasn't around to screw 'em up during their formative years, so they turned out just fine."

The audience laughed, and Jimmy continued.

"They can thank the families that raised them for that. I do. I thank them with all my heart. Wanna meet my kids?"

There was huge applause, and Jimmy looked into the wings where we were watching. He held up his foot with the hemp sandal.

"Hey," he cracked, "somebody stole my boots. No, not really. See these kicks I got on? They're moo-free and kind to the earth, and they belong to my son, Jesse. Get out here, Jess."

Jesse walked on stage as if he'd been doing it all his life. He smiled and waved to the audience. Someone yelled, "He looks just like you, Jimmy."

"He may look like me, but I wanna be like him. He's got a cool view of life."

Jesse gave Jimmy a thumbs-up, and the audience applauded.

"And now my other son, Gabe," Jimmy went on, as Gabe took a few steps on stage. He smiled at the audience shyly.

"We share a special bond, and you can bet he's gonna do something more important than I ever did."

Everyone clapped, and Jesse and Gabe walked back to the wings.

"And now my little girl, KT. She and I have a surprise for you."

I walked out and Jimmy motioned me over to the mike. What happened after that may have been a surprise to the audience, but it wasn't a surprise to me because we'd rehearsed that afternoon. Jimmy began playing a wicked rock riff, and "Big Dee" brought me my guitar.

I joined in with Jimmy on the riff, and the audience applauded. Then I began to sing the new song called "Handing Down a Dream" that my dad had taught me that same afternoon. He supported me with his guitar and encouraged me with his eyes. I pretended that it was just us alone, playing together the way we did in Malibu, which is what he had told me to do. Then, when I was sounding good even to me, I hit the chorus, and Jimmy began to sing with me.

The song exploded and the audience exploded with it. It felt as if the roof was going to come off the Forum. I looked out into the house. I could only see the first few rows, but right there in the middle of row one, a familiar face was looking up at me. His eyes were filled with love and pride. It was Dylan. He gave me an A-OK gesture and a smile that was impossible to resist. I couldn't help smiling back.

Jimmy and I soared and dipped and blended in that special way we had that was part of our DNA, and when the song reached its climax, we were deep in the pocket and wailing in perfect sync. We were so hot that the audience couldn't wait. They stood up for us right then, and when we reached the end, they roared their approval. My dad and I held hands and bowed and let the moment wash over us. He squeezed my hand and looked at me with such joy and love, I thought I would die from happiness.

⁂

After the concert and all the hoopla that followed it, everyone else was more than ready for bed. I was still pumped from the whole experience, so I wandered out onto the deck. The sky was velvet and the stars seemed close enough to touch. I was excited and happy and full of dreams and song ideas. Then I heard a whistle, and I looked down at the beach. It was Dylan.

I motioned for him to join me, and he raced up the stairs. We grinned at each other, and I hugged him without even thinking about it.

"Wow!" he said, hugging me back. "This is unexpected." I couldn't help but laugh at the happy, amazed look on his face.

Then he told me that Jesse had been texting him ever since the cantina. He had been kept up to date on where we were and everything that had happened to us, and he had always been close to me. He had, in fact, been the dude in the wet suit on the beach who had seemed so familiar.

We stood on the deck, leaning on the rail, watching the waves roll in and deposit their lacy, white foam on the sand.

Then Dylan took me by the shoulders and turned me to face him. He smiled down at me, and his eyes were dark and sweet and gentle.

"You didn't look at all nervous last night singing in front of all those people," he said softly. "Were you?"

"A little," I answered. "And then I saw you . . ."

He cut me off. "And you were too pissed to be nervous."

"I wasn't pissed," I told him. "I still don't know how I feel about you, Dylan, but my heart is open now."

"I'll find my way in," he whispered. "I believe amazing things can happen."

With that, he took me in those great guitar arms of his and kissed me, and that kiss tasted tender, sweet, and exciting at the same time, like a beautiful new beginning.

chapter thirty-one

The next day, my phone rang at six in the morning. It was Mom. This is what I heard (in no particular order) in her very loud mother voice: "Katherine Lambert, I cannot believe this whole Jimmy Savage thing. You are all over the newspapers and the TV. Are you all right? Where are you staying? How could you lie to me? Come home now! You and I have to talk."

It was 8:00 a.m. in St. Louis, and she had just picked up the morning paper. We were on the front page. The *St. Louis Post* showed a picture of the three of us on stage with Jimmy when he brought us all out for a bow at the end of the show. My mom, of course, called Sasha's immediately and Sasha broke under pressure and confessed everything. I couldn't blame her. She had her folks and my mom all coming down hard on her, and there was no way out of it.

"I'm okay, Mom. I'm in Malibu, California, at Jimmy's house. I'm sorry about the lie. We'll be on a plane soon, and I'll be back and in our kitchen by the time you get home from work," I told her. "Please don't be mad. I can explain everything."

"As long as you're okay," she sighed. "But prepare to be grounded for the rest of your life."

I staggered into the living room and Jesse, Gabe, Dylan, and Jimmy were already there. Gabe's folks were still at sea, but Jesse had gotten a phone call similar to mine. *Variety* was laying on the kitchen counter, and the headline read "Rocker Shocker Show Stopper." We were the hot story of the day. Chris was fielding phone calls from all the morning shows and wanted to know what he should do. It was an easy call. We decided right then and there that we weren't going to make any cheesy appearances or give any interviews to anybody. This all belonged to us and Jimmy and our families, and if we were to ever have our fifteen minutes, we wanted it to be about who we were, not who we were born to.

"Don't forget, your flight leaves in three hours," Jimmy told us. "I knew we'd blow our cover, but it was worth it. Now if you're all packed and ready, there's one more surprise before you leave."

When we had all gathered at the front door, Jimmy circled around us, herding us like a mother duck.

"Everybody ready? Everybody got their stuff? Close your eyes."

We heard the door open. "Now open them," he ordered.

We all gasped at what was parked in front of the house. Our ugly duckling clunker had turned into a swan. It was totally pimped out with a fresh silver paint job, black flames running up the side, off-road tires, new upholstery, touch screen GPS, and a hot sound system. To top it off, the custom license plate said SAVG KDS. Gabe was so blissed, I thought he was gonna pass out.

"It's for all the birthdays I missed," said Jimmy. "I'm driving you to the airport, and then I'm having someone drive it back to St. Louis for you."

There was nothing more to say, just lots of hugs to give. We had turned into a very touchy-feely family. I never, ever dreamed that could happen to me and my sibs.

⸸ ⸸ ⸸

Jimmy had a car waiting at the airport in St. Louis to drop each of us off at our houses. I was making a smoothie in the new blender I found on the kitchen counter when my mom got home from work. She tried to look tough and angry, but she was so happy to see me she just threw her arms around me and cried, and I hugged her with all my might.

"I'm not a rock star, but I love you very much," she whispered.

"I love you, too. I always did." I told her. "It just took me a while to find out how much."

"Who are you and what have you done with my daughter, KT?"

"I've decided I'm going back to Katie, Mom."

Mom hugged me even tighter. "Welcome home, Katie," she said.

"Being both parents is an impossible job," I whispered. "But you did it. Thanks for the birth."

"That was the easy part," Mom said, looking deep into my eyes. "It was my pleasure. You know, I've done a lot of thinking while you were gone, and you were right. Ken wasn't 'the one.' Neither were any of the others. When it is 'the one,' I won't be the person with all the feelings. He's going to feel as much as I do. It'll be something magical."

"You deserve that, Mom," I said.

"And I deserve an explanation from you, right now," she said. Her voice was serious, but her eyes were smiling.

I pulled out two glasses and split the smoothie.

"You're going to get every single detail. Hey, you got a new blender."

"I went out and bought it myself. It felt really good. Now, let me hear."

"I think you better sit down first," I said, pulling up a barstool. I started from the beginning, and she listened and sometimes she held her breath. And I know sometimes she was mad and sometimes she was scared, but sometimes she laughed and sometimes her eyes welled up. And by the time the story was over, we were hugging so hard that our arms ached.

"I'm incredibly proud of you, Katie," she said. "You've come a long way."

"So have you, Mom," I said. "I'm proud of us."

chapter thirty-two

A few weeks later, my brother Jesse invited all of us to a 908 family reunion at his house. I was so excited that I emailed Jimmy, telling him what was happening, all because of him.

Gabe, Jesse, and I had been talking on the phone, texting and emailing every day, but Gabe and I had the feeling that Jess had been keeping something from us. He told us that his moms had forgiven him for taking off without telling them, but there was something else he wasn't telling us.

Gabe had filled us both in on Joe's and Donna's reaction. He was scared that Joe would get all insecure because Jimmy was a celeb and all that, but Gabe underestimated his dad. Joe was what Sasha's parents called a *mensch,* a stand-up, unselfish guy. He was just plain happy for Gabe. Joe said he was the lucky one because he'd been able to be Gabe's day-in and day-out dad. And when the car was delivered, he was over the moon because he had planned to overhaul it, spiff it up, and give it to his son. Gabe thought he'd be bugged that Jimmy did it first, but Joe told him it was a first-rate job, and you can't argue with good work.

Donna just kept saying, "Thank god you weren't killed in that old heap," and hugging him every other minute.

When my mom and I got to Jesse's house for the reunion, we found that his moms had set up the backyard with a buffet and tables and chairs. They were chatting with Joe and Donna and greeted my mom and me with hugs and little spinach pies on a tray.

After a while, Gabe signaled to me and Jess that he wanted to talk to us alone. We sat down at a table, and he pulled a letter out of his pocket. The notepaper was imprinted with a small, yellow daisy at the top.

"Listen to this," he said. He sneezed into a napkin and began reading. "Dear Gabe, I'm sorry if I caused you any trouble, but I really needed that money to get started. I hope that you can forgive me for leaving the way I did, but I was beginning to like you so much that I was afraid I might cop out on my Hollywood career just to be with you. So I had to cut and run. Please understand, you are very special, and I will never forget you. Love, Daisy."

"I still hate her, just not so much," I told him.

"Hang on, there's more," he told us. "P.S. I hope you believe in your dreams. Mine came true."

He handed me the envelope, and Jesse looked over my shoulder as I pulled out three one-hundred dollar bills and a photo.

"The money is for you guys," Gabe said. "Check out the picture."

We did. It was a snapshot of Daisy and Miley Cyrus, smiling, their arms around each other . . . pals.

"Actually, we won it with her tip money. She didn't have to return it," I told Gabe. "She did that for you. To show you she really cared about you."

"She's right about dreams coming true," Jesse said. He nodded toward Liz and Tina who were overseeing the buffet table like a loving couple.

"They got back together in Barbados. They say it was because they heard the wedding vows. I say it was because they listened to them. I wanted to tell you about it in person," he said, beaming.

Just then, Dylan slipped his hand into mine. I hadn't seen him come in, but I felt his presence before he even touched me.

"You never know what amazing things can happen," he said as I leaned into him and put my head on his shoulder.

"He speaks the truth," Jesse added. "Get this . . . Jimmy is so into those hemp sandals that he set Willard up in the sandal business. Willard's got Horvard students weaving them by hand. They're called 'Soul Sandals' and Gabe, he wants you and me to help set up a website to sell them and donate half of everything to green causes."

"That is beyond cool," I told him. "It's so good to be with you guys. It wasn't until we connected that I realized I'd been kind of lonely my whole life, and now I'm not."

"Me, too," Jesse confided. "I never even knew it until I wasn't lonely anymore."

"I still don't have a girlfriend, but I'm not lonesome the way I was. It's because of both of you and Jimmy. I know it is," Gabe revealed softly.

We were all hanging out and having such a good time, we didn't even see Jimmy enter through the back gate, loaded down with flowers. The three of us spotted him, screamed, and threw our arms around him.

"I decided against the tattoo," I whispered in his ear. "Trying to make up for me?" he asked.

"No," I told him, "I think I'm being more of an individualist by not getting one."

We were still hugging and laughing when the parents lined up to be introduced. Jimmy presented Tina and Liz with a huge bunch of flowers, then another for Joe and Donna. And then he turned to see my mom standing a few yards away. He walked over to her with the last bouquet.

"I hope you're Kim," he said.

She smiled and nodded.

"Thanks for my girl child," he said, taking her hand.

"Thank *you*," she answered. "We did good."

He was still holding her hand.

"I don't want to let go," he told her.

"You don't have to," she answered.

It was a moment no one could miss. It was a real connection. It was magic.

Someone put Jimmy's CD in a boom box, and I spent that lazy summer afternoon laughing and talking and just hanging out with my brothers, my mom, my dad, and my extended family. I felt amazingly happy, and I knew I was going to use that feeling to write a song about the crazy, wonderful journey that had brought me to this place in my life.

That's my whole story, Donor Sibling Registry. I've never told it to anyone else. I'm officially giving you the okay to post the parts that you think will help other donor kids. And tell them all to remember what Dylan always says, because I really believe it now: "You never know what amazing things can happen."

THE END

about the author

Cynthia Weil is an internationally known lyricist with songs from "You've Lost That Lovin' Feeling," the most played song of the twentieth century, to the Oscar-nominated and double Grammy-winning "Somewhere Out There" from the animated film *An American Tail*. Her lyrics have been sung by the legendary voices of Barbra Streisand, Dolly Parton, and Kanye West. She has been inducted into the Songwriters Hall of Fame, The Rock and Roll Hall of Fame, in addition to receiving multiple Grammy nominations and two Grammy awards. It is only fitting, then, that *806: A Novel* has a teen songwriter as its main character. Cynthia's previous teen fiction, *I'm Glad I Did*, was published in 2015 to critical acclaim.

Currently featured as a character in *Beautiful: The Carole King Musical*, Cynthia resides in Los Angeles with her husband and songwriting partner, Barry Mann, and their dog, Callie. When not writing lyrics, you can find Cynthia fighting for animal rights, supporting young artists, or crafting her next book filled with music, dynamic relationships, and discovery.